BRIE'S SUBMISSION

Her Russian Knight

The sexy

Sadist

Red Phoenix

Red Phoenix

Her Russian Knight: Brie's Submission
Copyright © 2017 by Red Phoenix
Print Edition
www.redphoenixauthor.com

Edited by Jennifer Blackwell, Proofed by Becki Wyer, Marilyn
Cooper, Jennifer Roberts Hall
Cover by Shanoff Designs
Formatted by BB eBooks
Phoenix symbol by Nicole Delfs

Dedication

To every fan of Rytsar Durov – that sexy Russian sadist
we all know and love.
#TeamRytsar

To my beautiful fans who review every book and make
me laugh with their guesses about what they think will
happen next in the story,
You have my heart and gratitude.

While writing Her Russian Knight, a significant event
happened in our lives...
MrRed and I celebrated our 25th Anniversary!
This man is not only the father of my three beautiful
children,
He is my best friend
My lover
My soulmate
My confidant
My encourager
My inspiration
My Sir

YOU CAN ALSO BUY THE AUDIO BOOK!

Her Russian Knight #13

SIGN UP FOR MY NEWSLETTER
HERE FOR THE LATEST RED
PHOENIX UPDATES

FOLLOW ME ON INSTAGRAM
INSTAGRAM.COM/REDPHOENIXAUTHOR

SALES, GIVEAWAYS, NEW
RELEASES, PREORDER LINKS, AND
MORE!
SIGN UP HERE
REDPHOENIXAUTHOR.COM/NEWSLETTER-
SIGNUP

CONTENTS

Lea and the Dungeon

Rytsar woke up craving to play.

He walked down the corridors of the castle with a confident stride, his boots echoing pleasantly through the halls. He was impatient to release his sadistic needs and hoped he would be able to find a female from the wedding to succumb to his cat-o'-nine-tails.

When Rytsar entered the dining area, he surveyed the room of ladies seated for breakfast. Many were sitting in pairs, so he concentrated on those who appeared to have come alone. A few glanced his way and blushed when their eyes met, but it was Ms. Taylor who caught his attention as she leaned over, exposing her luscious breasts as she covered Brie's eyes.

He walked over to them and caught the tail end of her compliment. "...You were positively glowing when you entered the room. Are you already pregnant?"

Rytsar smirked, looking at Thane knowingly. The man exuded a sexual aura this morning that was impossible not to notice.

He could tell by the ravenous look in his comrade's

eye that Thane was currently imagining how he would position his new wife for the next fucking. Slapping him hard on the back, Rytsar said loudly, "*Moy droog*, I trust you made it count last night."

Rytsar appreciated the contrast from the smug look on his comrade's face and the expression of shock and disgust on the father-in-law's.

It was amusing to stir up trouble...

After listening to the heated exchange between Thane and Brie's father, Rytsar leaned down and whispered in Brie's ear, "*Radost moya*, I agree with Ms. Taylor. You do look particularly radiant today."

He was gratified by her stunning smile and turned his attention back to his comrade, saying with wicked sincerity, "If you should need anything—*anything* at all— I am here for you, *moy droog*."

Thane raised an eyebrow. "Rest assured, old friend, I have things under control."

Rytsar chuckled, taking Brie's hand and kissing it before excusing himself.

He decided light conversation was in order before he made the rounds of potential playmates, so he invited Lea to sit with him for breakfast. "Tell me, Ms. Taylor, did you have a pleasurable evening?"

"Did I ever! An entire castle full of hot Italian men? What isn't there to love?"

He nodded and asked, "I assume you sampled a few?"

She grinned but shook her head. "Actually, I didn't find what I was looking for. However, I had a whole lotta fun window shopping."

Rytsar looked her over with interest. "How do you swing, Ms. Taylor?"

Lea laughed, her eyes twinkling. "I'm open to any new experience. These days, the more challenging the better."

"And sadists?"

A red blush started from her ample chest and made its way up to her cheeks. "Well, I think my last dentist was a sadist. He insisted on giving me helium. I'd never heard of that being used at a dentist office before and asked him if it would help with the pain. Do you know what he said?"

Rytsar shook his head, staring at her intently, waiting for the punchline.

"He told me, 'No, but when you scream, it's funny.'"

Rytsar chuckled, picking up his fork as the waiter set down their plates. "Amusing."

"Hah, you think I'm kidding."

"Aren't you?"

Lea shrugged, a mischievous grin his only answer.

"So the question I have is…" He stopped, his forkful of meat only inches from his mouth. "Did you like it?" He winked at her as he enclosed his lips around the savory morsel.

Lea's wide smile showed off her pearly whites in answer to his question. "Just see how pretty my teeth are?"

Was the girl offering herself or simply teasing him?

"Mind if I break in?"

Rytsar was pleased to see Brie standing beside them. He was a bit jealous of Thane, knowing the wicked fun they would have on the isle during their honeymoon. For now, he would have to content himself with his fantasies centered on the *next* time they visited the island—as a threesome.

He offered his lap to the newlywed, since there were no extra chairs at their table, but when Brie told him she preferred to stand, he immediately stood up beside her. Lea followed suit, leaving him staring at her impressive cleavage.

Rytsar began imagining what he could do to those lovely tits, and barely followed the conversation until he noticed Brie staring at him sternly. "We calmed him down...no thanks to you."

He struggled not to laugh, secretly gloating that he had ruffled her father's paternal feathers. Putting his hand over his heart, he asked, "I only wanted to know if my wish to become a *dyadya* was now a reality."

Rytsar noticed Brie blush in pleasure.

The fact she might really be pregnant thrilled him. Rytsar had often been visited by the vision of holding her tiny child and being completely charmed by the wee one's smile. He experienced a pleasant stirring in his heart whenever he thought about the babe.

Placing his hand on her belly, he told Brie, "When tiny *radost moya* is ready to marry, I will not want to dwell on it." It was true—the thought of his niece being ravaged by a stupid boy someday totally enraged him.

With his hand still resting on her stomach, he asked with sincerity, "Should I go apologize to your father?"

"Oh, goodness, no!" She giggled. "You'll only make things worse by bringing it up again."

Rytsar smiled as he removed his hand, and leaned

down to growl in her ear, "Married life agrees with you."

He watched with satisfaction as Brie blushed a second time. Lea suddenly gave Brie a hip bump and announced, "The next time we see each other I'll either be collared or living in LA."

Rytsar's curiosity was piqued and he asked her, "Collared by whom?"

Lea looked at him with wide, doe-like eyes but didn't make a peep.

"Are you hoping to return to Russia with me?" he teased. He moved closer, trailing his finger slowly over the girl's throat. "I have yet to introduce you to my cat o' nines, Ms. Taylor. Shall we head down to the castle dungeon and see how it suits you?"

He could sense her desire and noticed as the rosy hue darkened on her magnificent chest. Oh yes, the girl was aroused by the proposition. "I see the idea excites you," he whispered huskily, his cock already hardening at the thought of chaining her up in the dungeon. "Come with me and we can test your limits."

"Although I'm curious…"

Rytsar was not going to take no for an answer. It was clear to him she wanted to scene as much as he did. He bit down on her shoulder, stating his dominance as he teased her senses.

"I can't," she gasped softly.

"But you can."

Biting her other shoulder, he felt her resistance crumble as her body surrendered to his will. It was going to be a satisfying session…

"Come, Ms. Taylor. Let's play."

Rytsar walked out of the room, knowing Lea was following behind. He was already mentally planning out his scene for her as they walked across the courtyard.

From behind him, she blurted, "Hey, so there were these two girls waiting to use the bathroom. The sadist ahead of them in line winks at them as he closes the door, telling the girls, 'This may take a while so enjoy the wait. I've got to shake hands with a dear friend of mine, whom I hope to introduce you both to later…'"

Rytsar shook his head as he continued to walk to the other side of the courtyard, knowing her joke was meant as a gift of sorts. Lea leaned on the comfort of silly banter, but he wanted so much more for her.

Opening the door leading down to the dungeon, he turned and warned, "Watch your step, Ms. Taylor. I don't want you to hurt yourself falling." He smiled hungrily as he leaned close and added in a lustful tone, "I want to be the only source of your pain."

Her little gasp set the sadist in him on fire. Today's session would be one to remember, there was no doubt in his mind, and he pondered why he had never played with the vixen until now.

Rytsar guided her down the narrow steps and through the hallway lit by torches all the way to the dungeon gate. The sound of the iron hinges creaking as he opened it for her added to the ambiance of their deviant encounter.

Two pillar candles on either side of a lone pole provided an eerie glow.

"Strip, Ms. Taylor, and kneel at my feet."

Lea immediately undressed, giving Rytsar his first

unencumbered view of those incredibly large breasts. Although they were surgically enhanced, her physician had done a remarkable job making them look natural and very pleasing to both the eye and groin.

Rytsar watched her kneel demurely at his feet, her head bowed and her palms open in submission.

"I need to retrieve my instrument. You will wait here until my return."

"Yes, Rytsar," she answered with bated breath.

With a wicked grin, he blew out the first candle and then the second, leaving only the glow from the light in the hallway to illuminate the room.

Rytsar closed the gate, letting it clink into place. He had no lock, but it was unnecessary. Ms. Taylor had the freedom to leave—but would she? Only her own self-determination and desire to scene with him would prevent her from walking out.

It was a test, and a lesson of sorts—if she was willing to learn from it.

He turned from Lea and slowly walked down the hallway, his boots echoing in the dark as he snuffed out each torch, leaving Ms. Taylor completely in the dark.

Rytsar took his time stripping out of his clothes. He slipped on his brown leather pants and put his boots back on, no other clothing necessary when scening with his 'nines.

As he gathered his beloved tool, Rytsar was struck by how fortunate he was. The submission of a woman in the hands of a sadist was a truly hallowed exchange. It was extraordinary to find someone not only willing to lay down their own desires, but to accept and embrace the pain he longed to offer—and he did not receive that gift lightly.

There was a time he had, under the tutelage of his father—a man who refused to recognize his submissives as thinking, spiritual beings. His father had taught Rytsar early on that women had been created solely for the purpose of fulfilling a man's pleasure. It never crossed his father's mind to appreciate a woman's submission, much less to thank her for it.

Hell, the great Vladimir Durov would not consider thanking a woman any more than he would thank a piece of steak for being succulent.

Having been cruelly treated by his father as a boy, Rytsar thought nothing of his callous treatment of submissives. It wasn't until college, when Rytsar witnessed Thane interact with the young sub named glee, that he realized his father had it all wrong.

That realization unbalanced his world—his whole way of thinking.

Now it seemed a tragic waste that he had personally whipped and fucked countless women with zero empathy or connection. How many of the girls had enjoyed his sadistic attentions, how many had endured it because of who he was, and how many had silently hated him for unleashing his pain on their bodies?

He'd never know the answer to those questions because he'd never once cared to ask.

Safewords were not employed in his father's circle.

In Vladimir Durov's mind, aftercare was a joke, emphasizing the weakness of any Dominant who dared to employ it. However, when Rytsar saw the connection between Thane and glee, and her growing adoration for his American friend, he realized that his father was a fool.

Although it took years to fully convert to a version of D/s similar to Thane's, Rytsar came to understand and embrace its raw power. When he started connecting with his submissives, he instantly noticed a change in his BDSM encounters.

While the subs had always taken an instant liking to him in whatever social group he was a part of, they now sought him out for private encounters. These women opened up themselves in ways they never had before because of the foundation of trust he'd established.

It allowed Rytsar to explore their limits more fully—taking him to heights he'd never experienced.

Truly, each encounter was like a small miracle. Although he had been born into violence, it had transformed into something exquisite when he scened with a submissive. They became his addiction of choice.

But the one thing he never allowed his submissives was entrance into his heart.

Tatianna was his only soulmate, and when she'd died, a vital part of him had died with her. He was incapable of love—or so he believed until he met Brie.

Radost moya was like a breath of fresh air. Knowing she was Thane's mate allowed Rytsar to draw close to her without any emotional barriers, and that ended up being his undoing. It had surprised him the day he'd acknowledged his love for Brie.

Rytsar had confessed it to Thane that very afternoon, when his friend had rushed to pick up Brie after the incident involving the maggot who'd tried to sell a young girl at the club. How strange that by killing that pathetic excuse of a man, the action had inadvertently sparked deeper feelings for Brie.

Rytsar remembered well the conversation he'd had with Thane that day…

"*Moy droog*, I am heartily sorry for compromising Brie's safety last night."

Thane cleared his throat, obviously troubled. "I trust those who witnessed it will never speak of it again. Frankly, I have no issues about what you did as long as it doesn't endanger her. At the very least, the reign of terror he caused ended last night. I can only hope the girl you saved survives this."

"The maggot needed to die," Rytsar growled in agreement. "Titov is watching over the girl now. He assures me that she is…adjusting. I can only hope. Mercifully, her parents fly in this afternoon, so I moved up her appointment for the medical procedure. No parent should have to see physical evidence that their daughter was treated like an animal." Rytsar spat on the ground.

Thane shook his head. "The evil people are capable of is truly shocking."

Rytsar glanced at his friend. "Both you and I have experienced it first-hand—at the hands of our own kin."

Thane snorted in response to the truth of his statement. Looking out the window at Brie, he said, "Thank God there are still good people in the world."

Rytsar knew the time had come to own up to his new feelings for Brie, but he was concerned how it would affect their brotherhood once Thane knew. "Comrade, I must confess that I am no longer infatuated with your woman."

Thane chuckled, glancing back at him and shaking his head. "What, she isn't masochistic enough for you?"

"She definitely needs more guidance in that area, but…I find it oddly attractive."

"What is it then?"

"I am in love with her."

If the news surprised Thane, it didn't show on his face. He stared out the window again, gazing at Brie tied to the tree in her furry boots. Holding up his glass to her, he said, "She is worthy of your love."

Rytsar clinked his glass against Thane's and they downed the vodka together.

Setting his empty glass on the table, Thane told him, "To be honest, old friend, I thought it would happen long before now. But then you've had your guard up ever since Tatianna, so it's understandable."

Rytsar grabbed the bottle of vodka and poured Thane another glass before filling his. "I did not expect it," he declared. "But when I took *radost moya* today it was different—*I* was different."

Thane turned his attention back on Brie and stared at her, saying nothing.

"What are your thoughts, comrade?" Rytsar asked when Thane remained silent, worried it had changed the dynamic between them.

Thane glanced back at him with a smirk. "When I invited you to play with us, I accepted this would happen." He slapped Rytsar soundly on the back. "It was inevitable, old friend."

Rytsar raised an eyebrow. "So we are still good then, you and I?"

Thane met his gaze before he spoke. "Of course. As far as I'm concerned, it's only natural that you should love her."

Rytsar chuckled in relief. Knowing their threesome encounters were not in jeopardy, he was struck by a divine inspiration. Snapping his fingers, he grinned at Thane. "I know what your wedding gift will be."

"Share," Thane demanded, looking at him with mistrust. "Practical jokes are not welcomed."

"*Moy droog*, I *promise* you will thank me."

"As long as it is not a gag gift."

"In this case, gags will not be required unless you insist."

"Well, hell…now you have me curious."

"And thus, the sadist in me is satisfied."

Thane grumbled good-naturedly, setting his glass back down on the table. "Why don't we take advantage of the submissive you tied so temptingly against that tree?"

"Let's," Rytsar agreed.

Mishka's Claiming

Entering the dark hallway to the dungeon, Rytsar lit the first torch, not bothering to relight the others. As he slowly approached the dungeon entrance, he heard soft weeping and smiled to himself.

Lea had stayed.

Rytsar opened the creaking iron gate, stating tenderly, "I'm here, Ms. Taylor."

"I…I was beginning to think you weren't coming back for me," she confessed tearfully.

Her earnest distress moved him. "Come," he ordered as he set down his bag of tools and slid the torch into place on the wall.

Lea stood up, the tears glistening on her cheeks in the firelight. He held out his arms to her, and she glided into them gratefully. Grabbing her tightly, he lifted her up and Lea wrapped her legs around his hips, silently crying on his shoulder.

"Shh…" he whispered huskily. "I would never abandon you, *mishka.*"

Lea attempted to hold back her tears but let out an

anguished sob in the effort. He could feel her terror and could only guess at the demons that lived within her.

"There…there," he replied gently, touched by her open emotion. Holding her tight, he whispered Russian words of comfort as she released the angst and terror being alone in the dark had caused.

"It is a worthy challenge to face your demons alone."

Lea nodded on his shoulder, still unable to speak.

"And because you were brave, you shall now be rewarded," he informed her, setting Lea down gently. He picked up the torch again to light the two pillar candles and the large candelabras set in the corners of the small dungeon.

The flickering of multiple candles filled the dungeon with a warm glow.

Rytsar turned to face her with a sexy smirk. "The light will allow me to better admire your marks."

"No, I can't!" Lea cried in a panic, then lowered her gaze to the floor and amended her initial response. "I'm sorry, Rytsar. I cannot have marks."

"Why the sudden change of heart?" he demanded.

"As much as I would love to wear your marks, I just can't."

"We do not begin unless you agree to wear them," Rytsar stated, staring at Lea intently.

He could see she was warring with herself, wanting what he offered but still afraid to give in to it. It was a common reaction with sadists.

"Where will you place them?" she asked in a hesitant tone.

"I will decorate your back and ass with my adoration."

He noticed her shudder and smirked to himself. Already she was imagining the burning caress of his instrument...

"Do you consent to my marks, *mishka*?"

Lea closed her eyes for a moment, but when she looked up at him again, she wore the confident look of a submissive who owned what she desired. "I would be honored to wear marks from the great Rytsar Durov."

He nodded his approval. "Have you experienced the cat o' nines before?"

"No."

"That pleases me," he said with a smile. Rytsar picked up his bag to open it, and grasped the handle of his 'nines.

He held the instrument out to her and ordered her to smell it.

Lea dutifully leaned forward to take in its scent. She looked at him in surprise but said nothing.

"What do you smell?"

Lea smiled shyly. "It smells like smoke, like an old-fashioned campfire."

Rytsar thought back to his mansion, which was *still* in the process of being reconstructed after so much time. Nothing was quick when the Russian government was involved. Fortunately, it was close to being finished because he had plans for the place—if Fate was merciful.

He'd lost practically everything in the fire that had destroyed his ancestral home, but at least this instrument had been spared, and it still carried the subtle aroma of its survival.

"Prepare yourself," he said with a wicked smile, "for I plan to challenge you. However, I require one thing."

"What's that, Rytsar?" she asked breathlessly.

He grinned down at Lea. "Your consent."

She met his gaze, her eyes luminous with fear. Glancing at his 'nines nervously, she asked, "What if I can't handle it?"

Rytsar swung the cat o' nines in the air, the sound of its angry tails cutting the air delightfully cruel. He smiled sweetly when he answered, "That's why you have the safeword, *mishka*."

Lea looked down at the stone floor, building up her courage. He waited patiently, knowing this encounter between them was inevitable. The moment she'd followed him into the dungeon, she had already made her decision.

After several moments, Lea finally nodded to herself and spoke up. "I trust you."

"My trusting *mishka*," he said with a tinge of sarcasm, his laughter dangerous and low. The ominous tenor of it caused goosebumps to rise on her skin. "While it is not misplaced, you may live to regret it."

Rytsar found it entertaining to mess with a submissive's mind during a scene. It kept her on her toes and focused exclusively on him.

"Go to the pole and face it with your hands held high."

As Lea walked over to the well-seasoned pole, the rise in her anxiety filled the room. She positioned herself as he instructed and waited, her breath increasing noticeably as he approached.

Rytsar thrust the handle of his 'nines into his back pocket so his hands were free to chain her to the pole. The ancient chains had a unique rattle as he secured the cuffs around her wrists. These iron restraints were misshapen and thick, attesting to their age and use.

While the dungeon now had the distinct honor of entertaining the Italian BDSM community, it wasn't that long ago people were imprisoned and tortured within these very walls. It gave the small dungeon a distinct and menacing vibe that Rytsar fed upon.

"First, I will reward you for your bravery. Then I will punish you for my pleasure."

She nodded, trembling when he stroked her bare shoulder. He growled seductively in her ear. "Have you ever orgasmed to Russian curse words?"

Lea smiled slightly, glancing back at him. "No, Rytsar, I can't say that I have."

Rytsar grabbed the back of her neck, grasping it tightly to assert his dominance over her. She instantly relaxed—like a tiny kitten being held by the scruff of the neck. The reaction was pleasing to the Dom in him because it spoke to her instinctual trust.

"I will murmur filthy things as you come, *mishka*." He trailed his fingers over her clit as he bit down on her shoulder. Already she was wet.

"Rytsar…" she whispered passionately, inviting his play.

He had to admit there was an alluring chemistry between them. Her feminine scent, which mixed beautifully with the lingering tang of her fear, drew him in. His cock stirred at the thought of her screams echoing down the hallway.

Rytsar pulled the cordless wand from his bag. Although the vibrator did not have the strength of the original wand, it was still capable of demanding multiple orgasms from a woman.

"I want you to be totally relaxed and sated," he growled in Lea's left ear, then switched to the other and added, "when the first stroke of my 'nines cuts across your back."

Lea let out a frightened gasp and then jumped when he turned on the wand, positioning it between her legs.

Rytsar took his time, slowly building up her initial orgasm. He leaned down and began his seduction of her, whispering foul things in Russian using a low, provocative tone.

"Oh...oohhh..." Lea cried out only a few moments later, already on the brink.

Rytsar pulled the wand away from her pussy. "Not so fast, *mishka*."

Lea groaned when he bit down on the sensitive part of her neck.

Rytsar backed away for a moment, wanting her body to come down from the edge it was teetering on. Crafting a well-orchestrated orgasm was almost a fetish for him. He derived great pleasure from a woman's climax, almost as much as fucking the woman herself. It seemed he had a unique talent for giving females memorable orgasms, and he utilized that skill to his full advantage as a sadist. It was the reason they kept coming back for more.

One of his submissives once confessed that his

knack for bringing unparalleled pleasure and following it up with addicting pain was like hot spice added to good food—one bite was never enough. Just as one night with Rytsar was never enough…

He returned to Lea, placing the vibrating wand back against her slick pussy. Nibbling on her shoulder, he focused on her climax, moving the tool away every time she tensed for release. After several minutes of purposeful teasing, he rewarded her.

Placing the vibrator firmly on her clit, Rytsar waited for her muscles to tense. Just before she orgasmed, he whispered lustfully the words 'you pain slut' in Russian.

"*Ty bol' shlyukha…*"

Lea began shaking as the orgasm took over, claiming her reflexes as well as her mind. He left the vibrator on just a few moments longer before removing it, knowing her clit was now unbearably sensitive.

It was important to keep her focused on the fact he was in control.

"Oh my God, my knees are so weak I can't stand," she whimpered, swaying in her bonds.

"You will come again for me," Rytsar ordered, placing the vibrator back on her clit.

"Oh no…" she cried, but quickly relaxed, willingly giving in to the intense vibration.

This time he slowly sank down on one knee to bite her on the ass. Lea shook as a second orgasm rocked though her.

When it was over, he stood back up and fisted her short hair, pulling her head back. "Are you ready for a new reality, Ms. Taylor?"

Lea looked up at him with fear and longing. "Yes."

"Very well." Rytsar released her and moved into position, swinging his 'nines to warm up. It was important to relax the muscles when wielding such a powerful instrument. One misplaced swing and you could permanently injure someone.

Rytsar watched Lea as the seconds ticked by—each one seeming more extended and drawn out the longer she was forced to wait for the first stroke.

Normally he started with a flogger and moved to the cat o' nines, but today he was feeling particularly wicked and horny. The only caress he wanted her to feel would come from these knotted tails. They would demand her focus, mesmerize her with their pain, and carry her to untold heights if she gave in to their cruel touch.

Rytsar cocked his arm back and let the knotted tails fly. When they fell against her virginal back, the shriek she let out called to his soul. "That was only a lick, *mishka*."

He let the next few strokes fall with the same power, crisscrossing the lashes on her back. Although a sadist, he understood the importance of warming up the body for more intense play. It was important that the experience be pleasurable for them both.

Already her cries had softened as her body acclimated to the bite and sting of his cat 'o nines. It allowed him to hear the seductive sound of the thud as each tail landed on her skin.

"Would you like it harder?" he asked.

"Yes," came her whisper just before she tensed in her bonds.

Rytsar smiled, swinging his 'nines close to her face so she would feel the cool air whip against her cheek.

She whimpered in surprise, expecting the shock of contact, and then broke out in giggles.

Oh yes, playing with subs was worthy entertainment: the creative control he was given could not be replicated in the outside world. This was his domain, he was ruler over every action, every reaction. Nothing could touch him here but the sweet cries of his sub.

Rytsar increased the power of his stroke just as Lea had instructed, and fresh screams filled the room, making his cock stir with lust. He watched her tremble, her entire back beaded in perspiration.

Was there anything more beautiful?

After several more strokes, he stopped and moved up to her, taking in the alluring smell of her fear and sweat.

"I yearn to challenge you further."

Her whole body shuddered when he touched her throat lightly and tasted her salty skin. Without waiting for her answer, Rytsar put the handle of his cat o' nines in her mouth and picked up the vibrator. He ran his hand down her thigh as he positioned it against her mound and turned the tool on. Her head rolled back slowly and she moaned as he began rubbing it against her wet clit.

Then he began to bite her throat, lightly at first. Her moans became panting gasps as he bit down harder and she came for him again, washing his hand in a flood of her excitement.

Rytsar let out a primal growl, biting forcefully as he

pressed the vibrator against her again, demanding yet another orgasm. Lea did not resist, crying out as the fourth orgasm claimed her.

He turned off the tool and asked her lustfully, "Do you accept my challenge, my courageous *mishka?*"

She nodded her head slowly, caught up in the sub-high overtaking her.

He took the 'nines from her mouth and kissed her gently on the cheek before moving away.

Rytsar could tell she was close to her limit. It was only her curiosity and desire to please that kept her from crying out her safeword. No one could know their true limits without being tested, and he thoroughly enjoyed playing that role.

Any sub willing to offer themselves to the sadist Rytsar Durov was going to be tested, and hopefully would come away from the experience more fully aware.

"You will remember this day," he told her solemnly as he readied to strike.

Two solid strokes, that's all he gave her, knowing that was all she could bear. Lea cried out in pain and began sobbing.

Rytsar put down his 'nines and returned to her, lightly grazing the new marks on her back. He smiled as he traced the angry raised welts he had created, having been careful not to break the skin.

Those marks would last a long time, as would the bite mark on her neck. He wanted her to remember her surrender to him—and to be reminded it of it every time she looked in the mirror.

Lea's sobs quieted as he began kissing her shoulder.

"I am a cruel Master, but I can be tender too, *mishka*."

His cock ached for her as he explored Lea's trembling naked body. "I lust for you," he murmured seductively. He unzipped his leather pants to release his hard cock before spreading her legs apart and pushing the head of his shaft against her drenched pussy.

She turned her head toward him slowly, her eyes luminous and glazed over with passion. "Claim me...Rytsar..." she begged, her speech slow and drawn out, an effect of the endorphins flowing in her veins.

In answer, he pushed the head of his cock inside her, closing his eyes for a moment to savor the erotic sensation of her hot pussy embracing the length of his shaft. It was a feeling like no other.

With his cock buried deep inside her, Rytsar unbound her wrists and placed them behind her back. Holding on to them for leverage, he began fucking her. He started out slowly, sinking his cock in deeply and grinding before pulling out. He wanted her pussy to be reminded repeatedly that it was *his*.

She moaned in pleasure, pressing her body against the pole to push her pelvis out farther to receive even deeper thrusts.

He began pumping her slowly, rubbing the ridge of his cock against her swollen G-spot. Using his calf muscles, he lifted himself to get a better angle, and her moans instantly became louder and more passionate. Knowing he had the right spot, he did not change the pace, but occasionally surprised her by pushing in to the hilt.

She was like putty in his hands as he built up her

next orgasm. When he was ready, he simply stayed still and relished the feel of her subtle pulsations before her inner muscles started contracting rhythmically, milking his cock.

Rytsar let out a low growl of pleasure.

Before her climax ended, he began fucking her again. However, this time he was not so gentle.

He forced Lea to the floor. "Hold on to the pole, *mishka*. You are about to be claimed."

Grabbing on to her waist with both hands, Rytsar began pumping his cock without restraint. All semblance of control left as he gave in to his sexual cravings and ravaged the girl.

The animalistic moans that came out of her mouth as he pounded her incited his more primal instincts, and he stopped for a moment to bite down on her shoulder. Lea cried out in ecstasy as she came around his cock.

Her powerful orgasm stripped away the last of his control, and he fucked her until he came like the beast he was. Nothing existed but the thrusting of his cock into her pussy until his entire body seized up just before he delivered a gloriously explosive come.

Rytsar screamed to the gods as his seed and all concerns were released in that singular moment. Afterward he grunted as he regained both his breath and his sanity.

He looked down at Lea's mottled back and smiled to himself. He'd done a fine job with her. The marks left on Lea's skin were beautiful and spoke to the level of connection they experienced during the scene.

After he pulled out and stood up, Rytsar moved over to his bag to fish out his ointment before snuffing all the candles out, leaving the two of them completely in the dark once again.

He returned to Lea and sat down beside her trembling frame as he began ministering to the wounds on her back, lightly spreading the healing salve over them as he spoke to her in the dark. "I have found it is cathartic to let the demons surround you."

Although he personally found it deeply cleansing, he realized it was not so for Lea when she began to tense beneath his touch.

"What are you frightened of, *mishka*?"

She let out a strangled sob. "I'm suffocating."

"What do you mean?"

"The dark…it's triggering…a memory," she told him between gasps, as if she were truly struggling to breathe.

"Go on," he encouraged, wanting to know the demon that held her captive.

"My parents…" She swallowed hard before adding, "They never meant—"

"Just spit it out. Do not qualify the memory."

She nodded, taking a few moments to try to rein in her fears so she could speak clearly. "I was only three, but the memory is still vivid for me." Lea whimpered.

"You must separate yourself emotionally from the memory, *mishka*, if you ever wish to be free of its power over you."

Lea only nodded, still too caught up in the memory to speak.

"Tell me what happened," he urged, gently stroking her face.

Lea stiffened, but he focused his touch on her temples, massaging those pressure points to help her relax. Soon she was able to share her thoughts out loud.

"My parents were running errands that day. I remember it was unusually hot outside." Lea took a deep breath, fighting off the fear. "They told me they would be gone for a few minutes, but they didn't come back. I watched for them as I started to burn up in the car. I kept fumbling with the handle, trying to get out, but it wouldn't open. Then I started hitting on the window, crying for my mommy. I couldn't breathe anymore…"

Lea started to gasp for air again as she relived the moment in her mind. "Every breath was like fire inside me," she said in a tortured voice.

Rytsar sensed she was coming close to suffering a panic attack and embraced her in his protective arms. "You survived, *mishka*. It's okay," he whispered.

He could feel the terror of the moment filling the air of the room. She buried her head against his chest and allowed the fear to roll past.

After several minutes, she stated in a voice hoarse with emotion, "My father told me that a good Samaritan rescued me from the car when he found me curled up in the backseat, my sweaty handprints all over the windows."

Lea started crying again, still haunted by the terror of that moment as a child.

"This memory…it lives like a monster inside you."

Lea rested her head against his chest. "Yes. Anytime I feel trapped, I go right back to that day and I can't breathe—I have to escape."

"If that is the case, I'm surprised that you consent to

bondage at all."

Lea pressed closer to him and mumbled, "Only with certain people."

"So I should feel honored?" he growled huskily, touched that she had been so brave with him.

Lea said nothing but turned her head and kissed Rytsar. She tasted of tears.

"Because you have shared your demon, I will acquaint you with one of mine. It's my belief that they have less power over you when you face them head-on."

Lea reached out to caress his jaw. "I want to believe that."

"Like you, my demons met me when I was young." He grunted as he allowed the unwanted memory to replay in his mind. "I was only five, but like you, it's as if it happened yesterday. My father was extremely angry at me, but I didn't understand why. I had done nothing wrong. He dragged me to a pole outside the servant's quarters while my mother screamed for him to stop.

"My older brothers...they just watched in stunned silence.

"My father was in a blind rage, bellowing like a bull as he stripped off my shirt and bound my hands without explanation. Then he served me five hard lashes from his whip."

There had been a time when Rytsar could still feel the physical pain of the whip, but he'd divorced his emotions and relegated it to a distant memory, now only recalling the facts without suffering the pain.

"After the whipping, my father told me it was not for a crime I had committed, but for an offense by my oldest brother, Vlad."

Rytsar remembered that day with extreme clarity because it marked the end of his childhood.

"I will never forget my mother's screams as the lashes rained down on her little boy."

"Why would he do that to you—his own son?"

Rytsar snorted angrily. "My father decreed that afternoon that I was the appointed whipping boy for the family. I remember the horrified look on my three brothers' faces when they heard it. No one took pleasure in my punishment except my father. He enjoyed hurting me, but being a sadist himself, I suppose that was to be expected.

"As time went on, and the shock of his edict became accepted, my brothers came to understand they were free to misbehave without consequence."

He let out a long, tortured sigh as guilt and anger washed over him. "I had wrongly assumed that when my younger brother turned five the responsibility would fall onto his shoulders. Although I felt sorry for Pavel, I was anxious to be relieved of the duty.

"I remember the day he was brought to the whipping post after burying one of Father's expensive pipes in the backyard. He was crying piteously, knowing what was coming, and all I felt was relief knowing this time it would not be me. But I was wrong.

"Father told my younger brother to stand beside the others and called me to the pole. When my mother protested, he had his men escort her away. I watched them drag her away kicking and screaming, knowing there was no hope for me.

"I refused to go to the pole, so my father grabbed me by the scruff of my neck and pulled me there, tearing off my shirt and binding me so tightly my wrist bled." Rytsar copied the harshness of his father's voice, saying, "Insolence will be doubly punished, boy."

Rytsar remembered well that particular punishment, but he'd only been able to endure part of it before he blacked out. He'd awoken to his mother's gentle hands as she tended his lashes while his father stood watch over him.

The man had glared down at Rytsar as if he was disgusted with his son. Whether it was because Rytsar had blacked out or survived the whipping, he was unsure. Fiercely defiant even as a boy, he'd met his father's scowl, unwilling to look away but secretly terrified of the man.

Rytsar tightened his embrace, confessing to Lea in the cover of darkness, "I always wondered what was wrong with me that I was the only one chosen to bear my father's wrath. What weakness did he see in me that justified my role as his whipping boy?"

Even now when Rytsar thought back on it, he felt a stab in his heart, not because of the physical abuse—no, it went much deeper. It disturbed him knowing there had been a time in his young life when he'd longed to be accepted by the brute—despite everything.

It made no sense and he felt shame for it now.

"I feared the man but longed for his love when I was a boy, but no longer. My rage toward my father is so dark, no light can penetrate it."

Rytsar abruptly lifted Lea up, releasing those unwanted feelings through the physical effort of lifting her. He felt for the matches and relit the first candle, filling the dungeon with its light.

"Life is full of demons, *mishka,*" he informed her. "However, we determine their power over our lives. Me? I won't be controlled by them."

Rytsar looked down at Lea tenderly. Her eyes were rimmed in red and her cheeks wet from many tears.

"I will finish tending to your marks up in my bed-room." He lit the torch with the candle and left her briefly to light the hallway before returning. Rytsar held out his hand to Lea and carefully lifted her, cradling her naked body in his arms as he carried her through the narrow hallways to his room.

Rytsar had learned in college, after observing Thane, that the care given after intense play was significant for both the Dominant and the submissive. While his own father scoffed at any man tending to a woman, Rytsar understood the importance. He'd experienced the bonding effects of it even as a boy, whenever his mother had tended to his wounds after each punishment.

Now, when he engaged in aftercare, it provided a tie to his mother's memory—a moment in time he enjoyed reliving.

Rytsar spent over an hour tending to Lea, knowing he had challenged her both physically and mentally. Lea's tan skin was the perfect canvas for the red welts he'd created. The color would remain long after the welts disappeared. He was particularly gentle in his care of her, and rewarded Lea for her courage with praise.

"I was unsure, Ms. Taylor, if you would remain after

I left you alone in the dungeon. Now that I know the fear you carry, I'm even more impressed."

"I almost ran, Rytsar," Lea admitted. "When the darkness closed in, the only thing that kept me there was telling myself that you'd come back. But when you didn't return right away, I became that little kid trapped in the car—abandoned and terrified."

"Yet you endured. Why?"

"I know that you are a sadist, so I forced myself to trust that this was simply a challenge and you had not abandoned me."

"You were wise to do so. I was not interested in scening with a curious child. I wanted only a fearless woman to wear my marks today." He smiled down at her. "And they look magnificent on you."

She smiled, looking at him in adoration. "You're not anything like I expected, Rytsar."

He chuckled. "What did you expect?"

"I thought you would be more…harsh and cold. I should have guessed that wasn't the case since Brie adores you so. But I must admit I've never met a sadist like you before." Lea giggled lightly, shaking her head. "You're kind—but exceedingly cruel."

Their shared laughter filled the room.

"Would you like me to tell you a joke?" she asked, her eyes sparkling mischievously.

"*Nyet*."

She frowned, looking surprised.

"But you may suck my cock."

Lea gave him a crooked smile.

"Graduates of The Center are said to be the very finest. And to think, I shall finally sample your skills at fellatio."

Lea suddenly burst out in a nervous giggle as a pink blush crept over her chest.

Her sudden discomfort made no sense and he questioned her on it. "Is something wrong, Ms. Taylor?"

Lea avoided his gaze when she answered. "It's just that... I...have someone at home."

He eyed her suspiciously. "You are taken?"

Her blush became an even deeper shade of red. "It's not like we're a couple or anything really, it's just that she..." Lea clamped her mouth shut and shook her head.

"I take it you prefer women," he stated matter-of-factly. Rytsar stood up and began putting on his clothes. "So we are done here?"

Lea looked humiliated, but only shook her head.

"It's fine. I had a pleasant time, I trust you did too."

"More than you know. You were...magnificent."

Rytsar raised an eyebrow. "Had you said otherwise, I would have known you were lying. Wet pussies tell no lies."

She giggled, but her eyes still conveyed her palpable unease.

"While I retrieve your clothing from the dungeon, you may use my bathroom to clean up," he stated, giving them both an easy out.

Rytsar left the room and headed back to the dungeon, shaking his head in amusement. "So *mishka* prefers pussy. Hmm... It explains why we never hooked up before, but it's a shame. She comes so hard around my cock."

Isle Dreams

Rytsar left Italy the next day, bound for Moscow. He'd enjoyed seeing his comrade marry, and trusted Brie and Thane would have a memorable time on their island.

Knowing he had a four-hour flight facing him, Rytsar let his thoughts drift to his friends on the isle. He might have to encourage those two to return to it in a few months' time. There were so many things he wanted to try with Brie—so many compromising positions he longed to put her in.

His cock responded to the mere thought of it and he had to adjust his growing erection. As he watched the rolling Italian countryside below, Rytsar decided to indulge in his fantasy.

The rumble of the puddle-jumper overhead alerted Rytsar to the fact his friends had finally arrived. He watched as the small aircraft landed near the island and the pilot helped Brie into a small boat.

Rytsar was surprised to see that Thane wasn't with her.

His curiosity piqued, Rytsar walked to the shoreline to greet them. Brie jumped out of the boat into the knee-deep water and took the suitcase the pilot handed her. She stumbled trying to keep the suitcase above her head as the waves crashed against her legs.

Amusing as it was to watch, Rytsar met her in the water, offering to take the suitcase from her.

"Oh, thank you, Rytsar," Brie exclaimed, just before a big wave hit and she fell into the swirling water.

Rytsar held out his hand to her, smirking as she grabbed on to him. Her clothes and hair were now sopping wet.

"You saved my stuff in the nick of time!" she cried, gripping his hand tightly as she threw her wet hair back. With his help, she was able to slosh through the moving waters and onto the shore.

"Where is your husband?"

Brie flashed him a shy grin. "He had a bit of business to take care of and said he will join us shortly."

"So I have you all to myself?"

"Yes…" she answered, suddenly looking anxious.

He placed his hand behind her neck and squeezed it firmly as he leaned down to kiss her. "Then I will make the most of this time." He released his grip and told her to follow as he disappeared down the path.

Brie giggled behind him as she struggled to keep up, her delighted laughter mixing well with the warm tropic air.

Rytsar led her to the small dwelling he'd specially designed for the island. It housed everything he needed, including the blue claw-foot bathtub. Of all the items in the tiny home, that had been the most expensive, mainly due to shipping costs. He hadn't regretted the purchase—it had acted as his calling card for Brie on the honeymoon, with its Russian scenery etched in the blue glass.

And now he would it put to good use...

He told Brie to strip while he readied the pole.

"I don't remember that being here last time," Brie told him as she undressed.

"Because it's newly installed, *radost moya*. Something I designed myself with you in mind," he answered with a wicked grin.

"Oh, so it's not just a stripper pole?" she teased as she knelt on the floor and bowed her head to him.

Rytsar smirked. "Oh, you *will* be dancing on the pole, but not in the way you're suggesting."

She glanced at the pole nervously while he opened a wooden box filled with custom attachments. With satisfaction, he fastened a large angled phallus to the steel pole, adjusting the level before tightening it securely.

He smiled at her. "Interested now?"

Brie nodded as he took out a second attachment, simple cuffs, and secured them at a level that would stretch her lean frame.

Once he was satisfied both were adequately secured, he opened his equipment bag and pulled out the Hitachi and a tube of lubricant.

"Lube the rod liberally as if it were my cock," he ordered.

Brie rocked gracefully from her heels and took the tube he offered before moving to the pole. It pleased him to see her curious and uncertain as she coated the large phallus.

He didn't miss the seductive way she used a twisting stroke on the tool as she lubed it, a direct result of her training at The Center. However, the fact she licked her lips nervously as she did so alerted him to her unspoken misgivings.

How daunting it must be for her—alone on the island with a sadist.

Rytsar chuckled to himself, causing goosebumps on her skin as she finished the job. He handed her a towel before giving his next command.

"Spread your cheeks apart and push that cock deep into your ass."

She stared at the instrument, her eyes widening as she contemplated its challenging size.

"Begin, *radost moya*."

Rytsar moved to a better viewpoint to watch as she spread herself open and positioned her pink rosette against the head of the toy. He gazed with interest as she began rocking against the device, willing her body to give in to its demanding girth. Brie moaned softly when the round head slowly slipped inside, stretching the delicate skin surrounding it.

"Very nice…" he murmured lustfully. He drew closer and began playing with one of her breasts as he watched the sensual progression of her efforts. She was determined to please him, but she did not realize yet that the phallus was actually a form of bondage. Once it was inside her, she would be immobilized and vulnerable to his every whim.

"Deeper," he demanded when it seemed she could take no more.

She held onto the pole behind her and used it as leverage as she forced it even farther inside, the length of phallus slowly disappearing into her sweet little ass.

"Well done," he complimented once he was satisfied with the depth. "Now raise your right arm." He took her small wrist and made her stretch to reach the cuff. He cinched it tight. "And the left."

She offered him her other wrist and he secured it, stepping back to admire her when he was done.

"Exactly what I envisioned. Your body stretched into a long, lean line…" He walked around the pole, looking her over appreciatively from every angle, "and your magnificent ass stretched taut with my instrument."

He ran his hands over Brie's skin, entranced by her soft femininity. He noticed she was breathing rapidly as her eyes followed him. His shaft responded to her heightened focus—and her growing angst.

Rytsar picked up the Hitachi and grinned at her. "Open your thighs."

Brie repositioned her feet to give him freer access to her pussy. She stared at the Hitachi with a look of excitement, knowing well the joy it could bring her.

But when he turned it on the highest setting, her expression quickly changed to one of worry.

"Oh," she whimpered when the wild vibration made

contact with her clit. She instinctually tried to move from its demanding intensity, but she was held in place by the phallus wedged deep inside her.

It wasn't until that moment that Brie finally grasped how truly helpless she was. Her look of surprise warmed his sadist's heart. Rytsar used more pressure on the wand against her clit and commanded simply, "Come."

Her thighs began to tremble, responding to the fierce demands of the tool. Few women could handle the higher setting, especially without an initial warm-up. That's where the challenge lay for her.

He enjoyed watching Brie struggle to make the decision to give in to the demanding vibration or be undone by it.

Rytsar observed her as he moved the wand slowly up and down her clit, relishing the inner battle playing across her face.

Brie's whole body began shaking as it fought against the intense stimulation while she mentally attempted to harness the wild vibration to incite an orgasm. There came a point when she had to close her eyes to concentrate.

With droplets of sweat forming on her upper lip, Brie broke through her own body's resistance and obeyed him, crying out as the first orgasm took over.

Rytsar lifted the wand from her so he could watch the muscles of her pussy contract in rhythmic movements, her overstretched ass muscles squeezing the toy buried inside her. The visual was a turn-on, so he opened his fly and began to stroke his hard shaft.

Without giving her body time to recover, Rytsar pressed the buzzing tool back on her clit.

"Please, no," she begged.

"*Radost moya,*" he said in a firm but teasing voice, knowing his little sub would not deny him.

Tears formed in her eyes as she battled for control in a situation where she had none. Sadism wasn't about dominating the body as much as it was about conquering the mind.

His will over hers…

For a second time, Brie gave in to his desire and forced her body to accept the challenging vibration. This time she screamed when she came, the effort proving almost too much.

Rytsar left the wand pressed against her clit a few seconds longer once the orgasm was over before turning it off.

Caressing her face, he said tenderly with only a hint of sarcasm, "Was it hard for you to obey me?"

Brie looked into his eyes, a shudder flowing through her body when he stroked her overstimulated clit with his fingers.

"Ahh…" she whimpered.

"Despite your obvious resistance, you're still very wet." He ran his finger over her slick pussy, and put it to her lips so she could taste her own excitement. "It leads me to think you enjoy my treatment of you."

Her eyes were glimmering with passion as her body trembled under his touch. "I long to please you, Rytsar," she said in earnest.

Rytsar undressed, his cock rock-hard and eager to penetrate her. "You are mine to play with as I will, and right now I want to fuck that hot little pussy."

He grabbed on to her thighs, lifting them up and

spreading her legs wide, her body pinned to the pole by the phallus.

Rytsar's cock was so hard that he had no trouble positioning it without his hands. He thrust into her wet opening as he looked into her eyes. The girl was so incredibly tight that he was forced to her enter slowly, like a virgin.

It took incredible self-will not to come at that moment. He paused to regain control before sliding back into her warm depths.

Rytsar was too close to last and gripped her thighs forcibly, readying himself to jackhammer her...

He heard the light knock before the door of his cabin slid open. "Pardon me, Mr. Durov. My name is Becki and I'll be serving you on this flight. Is there anything I can get for you?"

Rytsar looked up at the stewardess with curly red hair and could only smirk. There was no point in hiding his erection when her eyes were already glued to it.

"I can help with that," she offered with a winning smile.

When Rytsar nodded, she slid the door closed and daintily knelt between his legs.

He undid his pants and watched with satisfaction as she grasped his rigid shaft. It throbbed, needing release in her capable hands. Rytsar grunted as she began stroking him with a pleasantly tight grip.

"That is nice," he replied, "but your lips would be even better."

With a twinkle in her eye, the stewardess lowered her head. Rytsar closed his eyes as her warm lips enclosed the head of his cock.

"*Chyort voz'mi...*" he mumbled to himself, surprised how close he was to climax.

Becki paused briefly to ask, "What does that mean? It sounds so sexy."

Rytsar pushed her head back down, groaning. "It means 'Oh shit' because I am about to come." His balls contracted as he shot the first load into her mouth. To her credit, the sexy redhead swallowed each burst of come.

Afterward, he fisted her curly copper hair to pull her head back. She smiled up at him, wiping away a drop that had escaped from her lips.

It was good to be a Durov.

After the plane landed, Rytsar's instincts alerted him to the fact he was being followed while he walked through the international airport. Although he could not locate the man in the crowd, he knew with certainty he was in danger.

Rytsar was missing his normal entourage because of the personal nature of his recent travels, but he now regretted that decision.

Calling Titov, he quietly stated into the phone, "Do not meet me out front. I'm headed out a side entrance and will meet you on the lower level." He skirted past the flow of human traffic and disappeared down an unmarked stairway.

Just as he made it to the bottom step, he heard someone enter the stairway above him. Once outside, rather than wait for Titov to arrive, he started walking briskly in the direction the vehicle would be coming from. Luckily, he spotted Titov's car and was inside it before his pursuer made it out the door.

Rytsar unrolled the window and fisted his hand, giving the Russian equivalent of "fuck you" as they drove off.

"Definitely *bratva*," he snarled.

"It appears the brothers are calling in reinforcements," Titov agreed.

Rytsar felt raw, black rage boiling up inside him. "It seems you cannot alter fate."

Titov looked in the rearview mirror to address him. "But you must try."

Rytsar huffed, but he knew Titov was right. He was not the type of man to sit back and let others determine his future. He met Titov's gaze in the reflection. "I feel the need for liberation."

"The dungeon, then?"

"*Da*. The secluded one west of Moscow. I'll need to be more cautious now that the Kozlov brothers know I've returned to Mother Russia."

Rytsar texted a quick message and slipped the phone back into his pocket, trying to keep his emotions at bay. He could feel the walls closing in around him, as if the air was being sucked out of his lungs. It was only a matter of time before his past caught up with him.

He'd known it was inevitable, but he'd hoped for more time.

The Twins

Emiliya and missi were waiting for him when he arrived.

The naked twins bowed low as soon as he entered the private dungeon. They were just the distraction he needed at a time like this. Leaving all other thoughts behind, Rytsar embraced the control a scene with them would give him.

"I am in a playful mood today," he commanded, going over to the wall to decide on his instruments for their scene. Once he'd made his selections, he returned to the twins, tapping a rattan cane against his open palm.

The two brunettes turned to each other and smiled before returning their gaze to the floor. They answered in unison, "We are eager to please, Rytsar."

He liked their genuine enthusiasm, as well as the unique bond they shared as twins. Those sweet little masochists had a slightly sadistic streak for one another. It turned out they enjoyed watching each other receive his demanding attention. In fact, the sister watching usually orgasmed while he was playing with the other.

"Hold out your hands, palm side up."

They exposed their palms to him, holding their breath. Instead of striking the sensitive area, he simply placed the cane in their open hands without saying a word.

Rytsar walked over to one of the wooden bondage tables and pulled it closer to the other. The harsh sound of the heavy piece of furniture scraping across the stone floor echoed through the large space.

"Come," he ordered, gesturing to both tables.

The girls moved toward him, concentrating to keep the cane balanced and equidistant between them as they walked. Their care brought him pride. Tonight he would treat them to a scene they would not forget. He paused for a moment.

Was that to be his lot now? Treating each encounter as a final good-bye in case it were the last?

Rytsar shook his head. He couldn't allow himself to think that way or he might as well hand himself over to the Kozlov brothers now.

"Lie face down on the tables, heads turned so you are facing each other."

The girls giggled as they mounted the tables and laid themselves out, positioning their breasts in two cutouts designed so those beautifully sensitive pieces of flesh dangled freely, inviting play.

The twins then laid their delicate necks into the open metal chokers screwed into the tables, turning their heads toward each other with their cheeks pressed against the wood.

Rytsar secured the metal collar around emiliya's neck

and locked it. It was tight enough to prevent her from moving her head. Bound in this way, she was completely open and vulnerable to him. The only way of escape from his sadist desires would be her safeword.

He stepped back from her and asked, "Do you like the view of your sister I have provided?"

"I do, Rytsar," she answered, grinning at missi.

He tapped his cane several times under the table, teasing emiliya's nipples with the rattan. She squirmed as her sister looked on with pleasure.

Rytsar changed tactics, giving emiliya a sharp stroke on her ass, causing her to squeal out in surprise, the sting of the instrument bringing tears to her eyes.

Missi purred in excitement.

Grinning wickedly, Rytsar moved over to her. With sure hands, he bound her to the wooden table, feeling between her legs to confirm she was already aroused. "So you like seeing your sister squirm in discomfort, do you?"

"I do, Rytsar," she agreed lustfully.

"Let's see if she feels the same." He gave missi a quick stroke of the cane across her buttocks, making the flesh ripple from impact. Rytsar immediately followed it up with another stroke in the same spot.

Missi cried out, not expecting the double hit, but then she let out a long, satisfied sigh. "Oh, how I've missed this."

Heartened by her response, Rytsar danced the cane against her breasts under the table to the utter delight of her sister.

"Are you wet now, emiliya?" he inquired.

"*Da*, Rytsar…"

Rytsar moved to the back of the tables and began striking the bottom of emiliya's bare feet. She didn't react at first, trying hard to take it silently, but soon she was wiggling and whimpering.

"Be still."

Emiliya instantly froze and only made soft mewing sounds as he tapped the cane several more times on those pink, vulnerable feet. He then turned his attention on missi, giving her the same order to be still before tormenting her feet to the delight of emiliya.

Moving slowly up their calves, he savored his power over their increasing arousal. The twins played both observers and participants in this scene, and he—the Master over it all.

It was intoxicating.

Rytsar alternated between them as he continued up their thighs to their buttocks, choosing to spend extra time on those delectable asses. When both were decorated with pleasing peppermint stripes, he put the cane down.

"Please don't stop, Rytsar," missi begged.

The girls stared at each other, tears glistening on their smiling cheeks. They wiggled their hips in a desperate attempt to stimulate their swollen pussies. Greedy little cunts.

He chuckled as he left them to walk over to a chest of drawers. He slid the top one open and pulled out two realistic silicone dildos. His low laughter filled the space as he strolled back to his helplessly bound subs, who could only look at each other, unable to see what he had in mind for them.

Rytsar stood between the two tables with his hands behind his back. "Open your legs wide so I can see how swollen those pussies are."

The twins did as he asked, glancing nervously at him, hoping to read on his face what he intended to do.

For his own amusement he gave them a harsh look, which made them shudder in fear.

"Who wants to go first?"

"Emiliya does," missi volunteered.

Rytsar turned to emiliya. "Which do you prefer, dark cock or light?"

Her eyes widened. "I love yours, Rytsar."

"Good answer," he replied with a satisfied smirk. "Since your sister was so quick to volunteer you, I think she should go first."

Emiliya grinned at her sister. "If it pleases you, Rytsar."

He placed the dildo she'd requested down on the table beside her so she could anticipate having it stuffed inside her, then he moved over to missi.

Missi whimpered, biting her lip when he pressed the large head of the hefty dildo against her wet pussy. He began thrusting it slowly, watching her body eagerly embrace its girth.

"I'm fucking your sister with a big black cock," he growled huskily.

"Ohh…" emiliya cried beside him, squirming as she watched her sister's expression as Rytsar forced the phallus deeper. Missi let out a passionate moan, causing emiliya to squirm even more. Once it was wedged deeply inside, he slapped missi on the ass and moved over to emiliya.

The girl's eyes were transfixed on the huge dildo that was soon to become her silicone lover.

"Kiss it," he demanded, holding it close to her mouth. Emiliya pressed her lips against the head of it with a mischievous smile.

Her sensual kiss was a turn-on, and a rush he felt instantly transferred to his groin. Tonight he was intent on keeping control for the long session. He moved the dildo away from her beautiful lips and positioned it against her "other" lips.

Keeping his gaze on emiliya's face, he eased the dildo into her. She was looser than her sister, which meant he could challenge her more with the instrument. Gritting his teeth, he thrust the phallus, enjoying her look of surprise at the depth.

Missi started panting loudly as she rolled her pelvis against the table, using the pressure of the dildo inside her to increase her pleasure as she watched Rytsar pound her sister with the huge phallus.

When it appeared that emiliya was about to orgasm, Rytsar immediately stopped.

He left her panting in need as he went over to the wall to get two floggers. Tonight would be an extended session of cruel temptation, pain, and denial. He was in a particularly devilish frame of mind, and wanted to explore their limits far more than he had in the past.

By the end of the evening, not only would the twins know each other on an entirely new level, but they would know just how exceptionally creative he could be...

Light in His Darkness

Sleep had become a fickle mistress since Rytsar had returned to Russia.

He often found himself awake at that odd time between the death of the last day and the birth of the next. That strange hour when the world seemed to stop for everyone except the insomniacs. Rytsar used to fight it, but now he embraced it. Living on borrowed time made every second precious.

But he was growing tired, unsure if fighting the inevitable was worth it.

He'd just settled down in his favorite chair with a shot glass and a bottle of vodka beside him. In times like these, vodka was a good and faithful friend.

Rytsar's phone buzzed on the end table so he picked it up, curious who would be texting him at such a strange hour. The picture that popped up on the screen surprised him. It was a bottle of Zyr vodka surrounded by a red circle and a diagonal line through it.

"It can't be…" he muttered to himself in disbelief. He immediately dialed Thane's number and shouted,

49

"I'm a *dyadya*!"

"It's true, old friend," Thane chuckled, affirming his claim.

"So you finally made your fucking count."

Thane sounded mildly irritated. "Need I remind you that we *just* got back from the honeymoon?"

"*Radost moya* would have been pregnant the day of the wedding if it had been me," Rytsar declared.

He heard Brie giggle in the background and he felt light enter his heart. "How are you feeling, *radost moya*? Are you nauseous? Do you need to come to Russia so I can tend to you?"

She laughed, assuring him that she was feeling perfectly fine.

"Is it a boy or a girl?"

Brie answered by calling the babe a "zygote" and insisting it was simply a bunch of cells at this point.

"You and your scientific words," he scoffed. The wee one she now carried had brought hope back into his life—a ray of sunshine in the dead of night—and he told her, "You're pregnant with *moye solntse*."

"What's *moye solntse*?"

"It's her name, *radost moya*," he explained tenderly.

He heard Brie whisper something to Thane who answered with "my sunshine"—the meaning of the name in English.

When she spoke again, her voice trembled with emotion. "I love that name, Rytsar."

"You do realize we may have a boy, old friend," Thane asserted.

Rytsar only laughed. It was fine that his comrade was

being an idiot, because Rytsar knew Brie was carrying a girl. He would stake his life on it.

Unfortunately, Thane's response caused Brie concern and she asked Rytsar, "You will still love our baby if it's a boy…won't you?"

Rytsar was hurt by her question and replied firmly, "I will love your child."

He could hear the relief in her voice when she said, "Good, because you're going to make a wonderful uncle."

"*Dyadya*," he corrected, knowing he would love and spoil little *solntse*.

"*Dyadya* forever and always," Brie affirmed.

A tear came to his eye at the thought of holding the wee babe in his arms. He could see her, he could even feel the weight of her cradled in his embrace. It was fated that he would live to hold that child, and it gave him a renewed sense of purpose.

Out of curiosity, and a need to confirm where he stood, Rytsar asked, "Who else has been told, comrade?"

Thane was quick to answer. "Just Brie's parents and my Unc," but then there was a paused before he added, "Oh, and Nosaka."

Rytsar couldn't believe it. Why on earth would Thane tell Nosaka before him? Had the world gone completely mad?

"What?!" he roared into the phone.

Thane's amused chuckle let Rytsar know he'd been played.

Now I'm the fucking idiot.

"Oh, so you jest, comrade?"

When Brie laughed too, he felt doubly chagrinned.

"Sorry, Rytsar, but that *was* funny."

Trying to save the last shred of his dignity, Rytsar replied, "Fine, you two can have your laugh at my expense, as long as I am named the godfather."

"We're not striking deals here," Thane countered.

Rytsar was aghast and insisted, "It is only right as your brother."

Thane seemed to understand he'd pushed too far with his kidding, and said, "We will discuss those things at a later date. Right now you need to go back to sleep and we have other calls to make."

Did his comrade really think he was going to sleep after this wonderful news?

"*Radost moya*, take care of yourself and the babe," Rytsar said compassionately, wishing he was with her now to celebrate.

"I will, Rytsar."

To his brother, he said with all sincerity, "*Moy droog.* You have made me a happy man."

After hanging up, he placed the cell phone on the arm of his chair and poured himself a shot. He held the glass up and stated to Fate, "I will hold that child in my arms, and nothing you do can stop me."

Swallowing down the welcomed fire, Rytsar smiled to himself. How truly miraculous life could be. One moment he was on the verge of conceding defeat and the next *moye solntse* arrived to save and inspire him.

It was possible life wasn't as dark as he'd assumed.

With renewed conviction, Rytsar called Titov. The man was quick to answer the phone, but it was obvious by his slow speech that Rytsar had woken him from a deep sleep.

"I need you to come. I just received news that changes everything."

Rytsar planned go into hiding until the babe was due. No one would be able to find him—not even God Himself. He looked down at the ancestral ring on his finger, ashamed now that he'd been so close to forfeiting his life.

He was a Durov. He came from a long lineage of warriors. Whatever it took, whatever sacrifices he was forced to make, he would live to see *moye solntse* take her first breath in this world.

Rytsar hadn't appreciated what a big sacrifice total isolation would be until he had to live it day in and day out.

Being secluded from the world for an extended amount of time was like being a lion stuck in a small cage. Extreme boredom with no means of escape.

He began to feel fidgety after only a few days, pacing through the rooms with nervous energy and no hope of relief. Breaking his forced silence to preserve what little sanity he had left, Rytsar attempted to contact Thane but was only greeted with his damn voicemail.

Likely, it was his comrade's lame idea of a joke, knowing how excited he was about the babe, and sure...he might deserve it for the many inspired pranks he'd played on Thane throughout the years.

Still, the timing of it couldn't have been worse for him and only made Rytsar that much more unsettled.

Not wanting to endanger his friends, Rytsar had purposely kept Thane in the dark about how serious things had become. He fully expected to receive shit for it when the truth came out and Thane learned of his deception, but Rytsar stood behind the decision.

It was necessary—*nyet*—essential, that neither Thane nor Brie were involved. While he did not regret ending the life of the maggot, it bothered him that Brie had been there to witness it.

He hoped, someday, Thane would come to understand that his silence was only out of a need to protect them from the consequences of his actions that night. Up to this point, Rytsar and Thane had been painfully open with each other. Their blood bond demanded full disclosure. He was deeply concerned at Thane's reaction when his lies of omission were revealed, but it was his solemn duty and joy to protect Brie—and now little *moye solntse.*

Rytsar grinned just thinking about the babe.

In nine months' time, he would be holding the tiny girl in his arms. It made anything he had to endure bearable. To imagine Brie with the blush of motherhood did his heart good. She was meant to be a mother, and Rytsar was grateful Thane had finally agreed to giving her that opportunity.

Until Brie, he'd never have guessed his comrade would willingly become a father. Thane had been adamant that the kindest thing he could do for a child was never to have one.

However, Rytsar had always maintained that Thane would make a good father, just as he made an excellent trainer. His insight and wisdom would help guide his parenting when emotions failed him, and with *radost moya* by his side, the child would never want for love.

It was good that Fate was challenging Thane in this way. He would become a better man for it. And it was fortunate for Rytsar that he would reap the benefits of being a part of the miracle without having to add any complication to his own life.

Rytsar turned on his sound system and turned the dial up high. Closing his eyes, he forced himself to concentrate on the music. With vodka and classical music as his allies, he would survive this unwanted exile.

Suddenly, he felt a presence in the room and opened his eyes to see his attacker approaching. With the reflexes of an assassin, he pounced on the man and pulled back his arm to deliver the killing blow.

"Rytsar! Rytsar, it's me!" Titov screamed.

Rytsar paused with his fist in midair, but it took several seconds before his body registered what his mind had already processed. He slowly lowered his arm and rolled off Titov. "You nearly killed yourself coming in unannounced," Rytsar growled.

"I called out before entering, but you couldn't hear me."

Rytsar stood up, eyeing the man reproachfully as he went to turn down the music. It scared him how close he had come to ending Titov's life. "Why are you here? You know that this could compromise my cover."

Titov held out an envelope, his expression grave. "This was sent to your main residence."

Rytsar snatched it out of Titov's hand, demanding, "What, is this a formal threat from the Kozlovs? Why the hell would I care?"

Titov met his anger with a look of sympathy. "No, comrade."

His reaction set Rytsar on edge. Pulling out the telegram, he read:

Rytsar Durov,

Please forgive the lateness of this message. Thane Davis was involved in a plane crash and remains in critical condition. Due to an unfortunate error, you were not contacted until now. Mercifully, he continues to shows signs of improvement.

Sincerely, Ren Nosaka

Rytsar stared at the note, frozen as the news slowly filtered its way to his brain and a cold chill coursed through his body.

No…

He'd lost too many—he wouldn't survive the loss of Thane.

Rytsar closed his eyes as images of Tatianna's and his mother's lifeless eyes flashed before him.

Shaking his head violently, Rytsar tried to force those demons of his past at bay. He hadn't been able to save Tatianna—or his mother—and a feeling of inevitability crept through his veins. Thane was destined to die.

Rytsar was a cursed man. Everyone he'd ever loved met with an untimely death.

Struggling to keep his composure as he stared at the note, a new feeling overpowered his sense of doom as rage took over.

He stared at the name Ren Nosaka. How ironic that the Kinbaku Master was the one to inform him of the accident, and how convenient it was long after the fact. Had the Asian Dom been "caring" for Brie the whole time Thane lay dying in the hospital?

How long had that bastard purposely kept Rytsar in the dark?

Had it been days—or weeks even?

Rytsar thought back on how long he'd been unable to reach Thane and suddenly felt ill. It hadn't been some kind of pathetic joke on Thane's part. No, his comrade had been fighting for his life all this time.

There could be no other explanation for Nosaka keeping Rytsar away other than to claim Brie as his own the minute Thane passed.

Knowing the Asian Dom had deep feelings for Brie, had even expected to collar her the night of her graduation, made him a threat. Thankfully, *radost moya* had realized who her true Master was—although Thane had tried to deny it when she'd offered him her collar.

The more Rytsar thought about it, the more enraged he became.

How dare Ren Nosaka try to fuck with their lives like that! The bastard was worse than a vulture, standing on the sideline waiting for Thane to take his final breath so he could swoop down to claim Brie and little *moye solntse.*

Rytsar began to see red.

If the worst happened, and his comrade passed from this world, he would never let Ren Nosaka collar Brie—never.

But the thought of Thane dying instantly brought a physical pain so great Rytsar clutched his chest.

I cannot lose you, brother…

Rytsar barked out his orders to Titov. "Secure the plane in route and gather my men. We're leaving this instant."

He didn't bother packing, grabbing only his wallet and his cell phone before heading out the door.

"I'm coming, *moy droog*," he muttered. "Don't you dare leave me."

To survive the unbearable length of the flight from Moscow to Los Angeles, and bury away the dark memories of his past, Rytsar slipped on a pair of headphones and closed his eyes. He listened to the song "O Fortuna" repeatedly for the next twelve hours.

It was the only way to keep his mind from wandering to places he dare not go.

The moment the plane rolled to a stop at the LAX terminal, he pushed the pilot to open the door so he could exit. There was a vehicle waiting for them. His driver understood the urgency of their mission and sped to the hospital at the risk of getting caught breaking the law.

Rytsar knew, even if the police attempted to pull them over, his man would not stop until they reached their destination. His men were loyal to him, no matter the consequences to themselves.

Before the vehicle came to a full stop, Rytsar jumped out and pushed through the hospital doors with his entourage following behind him. He immediately approached the front desk and demanded to know where Thane was.

The flustered woman stumbled over her words, looking at all the intimidating men. "Mr. Davis? Umm…let me see. It looks like he's in the ICU."

"Where is that?" Rytsar demanded.

"It's on the fourth floor. But only close family members are allowed in…"

"Thank you." Rytsar started toward the elevators but decided to take the stairs instead, running up the steps two at a time. Not about to be stopped, he barreled his way into the ICU, ignoring the nurses who tried to stop him.

Rytsar was not surprised to find Nosaka in the room with Brie, but became incensed when he found her in the arms of the Kinbaku Master with the man gently stroking her hair.

With nostrils flaring, Rytsar rushed in and headed straight for the man. "Get your hands off her! I am the brother. I should be caring for *radost moya*—not you!"

Rytsar grabbed his shirt collar for leverage, and fist connected with jaw. He held back the power of his swing only out of respect for Brie.

Nosaka fell to the ground with Brie crying out behind him in desperation, "Don't hurt him, Rytsar!"

Falling to her knees beside the traitor, Brie moved in to shield him from Rytsar's wrath—which only incensed him even more. Pointing to Nosaka, he roared, "No one touches *radost moya*—least of all you!"

Nosaka was unsteady on his feet as he stood back up and claimed, "You've got this all wrong."

Like hell I do! Rytsar thought. He turned his attention on Brie and demanded angrily, "Why didn't you contact me the minute the plane went down?"

She looked genuinely devastated when she answered. "I'm so sorry, Rytsar... I didn't know you weren't contacted until a few days ago."

"I left messages on Thane's phone that went unanswered," he told her. Suddenly the dam of emotions he'd been trying to hold back began to crack—and his voice caught. "I thought he was playing some kind of joke."

Rytsar walked over to Thane. His friend's eyes were open but he was staring ahead with no spark to be found in those windows to his soul. It seemed Rytsar's worst dreams were coming true.

"*Moy droog...*"

He'd seen that lifeless stare with his mother just before she took her last breath.

The dangerous tempest of the past swirled around this new source of pain. With herculean strength he held it back, but he could not stop the tears from welling in his eyes.

Brie came up beside him, explaining gently, "He still remains in a coma."

"But his eyes..."

"They're open but the doctor says he's still unconscious."

He let the tears fall when he put his hand on Thane's shoulder. Rytsar should have been here the very day it happened. His brother should not have had to fight this battle alone. "How long you've been suffering, comrade…" he choked out.

Brie attempted to assure him. "I've done everything I can think of to keep Sir stimulated and comfortable."

Rytsar could barely force out the words when he asked again, "Why didn't you call?"

Her bottom lip trembled when she answered. "I had no idea you hadn't been reached. I'm so sorry."

"I would have come as soon as I heard. Surely, you knew that."

Brie's confession pulled at his heart. "I've tried so hard to be strong on my own."

However, Rytsar felt his deep-seated rage resurface again. "And yet you let this man stand in for me?"

She bravely met his anger head-on, correcting him. "I didn't ask Tono to come. Master Anderson did."

His fury suddenly shifted to Brad. "Where is that traitor?"

Rytsar felt Brie's gentle touch on his arm, and for a brief moment he relaxed enough to hear what she was saying.

"Master Anderson kept me safe before the car accident."

What the hell? Has the entire world turned upside down?

"What car accident?" Rytsar demanded.

"Master Anderson's truck was totaled, but thankfully

he only suffered a broken leg in the crash."

Good, the traitor is still alive and will be made to pay.

Slamming his fist into his palm, Rytsar declared, "I will add a few more broken bones."

"No!" Brie cried. "Master Anderson's been nothing but kind to me. Both men have."

Rytsar looked at Nosaka, feeling nothing but anger and distrust. "You have no business caring for *radost moya*."

God only knew what the man had done with no one there to stop his advances on the girl.

"Get out!"

When Nosaka made no move to comply, Rytsar had to fight back the urge to punch him a second time. He warned ominously, "Get out of here, Tono Nosaka."

The Kinbaku Master finally responded to the threat in his voice and exited the room, despite Brie's protests for Nosaka not to leave.

Rytsar watched with interest as the man blocked the security guards from coming into the room to haul Rytsar away. Instead, Nosaka convinced them to return to their posts. It surprised Rytsar, but did not sway him.

Once the Asian Dom was gone, Rytsar wrapped Brie in his protective embrace. All the furious tension dissipated the moment Brie began to sob in his arms.

"Oh Rytsar…"

He lifted her up off the floor and held her against him. The intense sorrow flowing between them melded into a black ball of grief. In that melding, they were able to draw strength from each other. When he regained the power of speech again, he asked her, "How long has it been?"

"About a month and a half," she said with a sniffle.

Rytsar nodded, knowing he'd been right. He carried her over to Thane's bed before setting her back on the floor. Together they stared down at his motionless body. The tick of a large clock behind the bed counted out each passing second.

"I'm so sorry, *moy droog,*" Rytsar whispered, fighting off the emotions and fear when he realized that there was a good chance that even if his comrade were to regain consciousness, he would not be the same man.

In truth, Rytsar may have already lost his brother.

He looked down at Brie, and a new flood of emotions washed over him as his gaze lowered to her belly. Whatever happened, he would take care of the child. Brie would always have his full support.

Rytsar laid his hand on her belly. "Is *moye solntse* okay?"

Brie looked down at his hand and smiled. "Yes. In fact, I go in for another check-up in a couple of days." She gazed up at him. "Would you like to come?"

For the first time since receiving the terrible news of the crash, Rytsar felt a glimmer of light. "I would be honored to attend in my comrade's place."

He looked back at Thane with regret, hating this new reality they found themselves in.

"The doctors told me that Sir can hear us, so I've been talking to him as if he is aware of everyone in the room."

Rytsar narrowed his eyes. "If that is true, then what was that exchange I witnessed when I walked in just now? It did not seem you two were behaving as if Thane were here."

She bristled at his accusation, but he was not sorry he'd voiced it.

"You have no idea what you are talking about. I woke up this morning believing Sir would wake up today. I was certain of it." She looked down at her husband and frowned sadly. "I was devastated when I came in this morning and nothing had changed." She met Rytsar's gaze. "What you saw was Tono telling me not to lose hope."

Rytsar furrowed his brow in disbelief. "Are you telling me that man hasn't made any advances toward you?"

Brie's gaze did not waver. "He has been nothing but respectful to me *and* to Sir." She started shaking her head, tears coming to her eyes. "Tono didn't deserve your anger, only your deepest gratitude."

Rytsar snarled. "Then why didn't he contact me sooner?"

"I told you, neither he nor I had any idea you didn't know until I got Sir's phone back and was able to listen to the messages. As soon as Tono knew, he tracked down how to reach you, because neither of us were able to leave a message on your cell."

Rytsar's anger toward Nosaka began to diminish, but he was still furious about being left in the dark. "Why did Brad call *him* instead of me?"

Brie looked up at Rytsar, shaking her head. "I don't know." She wrapped her arms around him. "But I'm glad you're here now." Placing her head against his chest, she murmured, "I have missed you, Rytsar. I know Sir has, too."

Rytsar grunted in response, the feelings of love and loss overpowering for him. He stared at Thane as he held Brie in his arms.

Are you really here, brother?

For the briefest moment he swore he felt Thane's presence beside him. But just as quickly as the feeling came, it disappeared.

"He's trapped," he told Brie.

She looked up at him. "I think so, too, and I've tried *everything* I can think of to bring him back."

Rytsar leaned in close, just inches from Thane's face, and stared into those blank eyes. "I feel your spirit, *moy droog*. Keep fighting."

There was no change in Thane's expression. After several moments, he turned back to Brie and announced, "We will find a way to set him free."

Brie nodded, smiling awkwardly as she tried to stop more tears from falling.

Rytsar could not bear to see her cry when he was close to breaking down himself. "Do you want me to apologize to Nosaka then?"

"Yes," she answered, dabbing at her eyes.

He hated to leave Thane even for a second, but knowing he'd upset Brie by misreading Nosaka's actions bothered him. "Brother, I will be back soon."

"Do you want me to go with you?"

"*Nyet.* Stay with your man. He is more important."

Brie pulled out her phone. "I'll inform the doorman to let you in." She handed him her apartment keys with a grateful smile. "I felt something big was going to happen today. I just never suspected that big thing would be you."

Rytsar gave her a kiss on the forehead before heading out. He could feel the guarded stares of the hospital staff as he walked out of the room. In truth, he had no issues with them being afraid of him—fear was a powerful ally.

Unlikely Ally

Before he left, he told two of his men to stand guard outside the doors of the ICU. Once on the road, he rattled off instructions to Titov. "Ready the beach house, but inform the extra guards to remain inconspicuous. I don't want her to be concerned."

As soon as he entered the apartment, Rytsar felt a stab of pain in his chest. This place held so many good memories, but it seemed empty and hollow now.

Rather than dwell on it, he called out loudly, "Nosaka!"

The Asian Dom came out from the guest bedroom and met Rytsar's gaze, approaching with caution.

Rytsar stared at him, unsmiling. He could read in Nosaka's eyes the truth he'd refused to acknowledge earlier. The man was genuine—and could be trusted.

Grabbing Nosaka with both hands, Rytsar hugged him hard, purposely holding him longer than necessary. Stating his dominance over the Kinbaku Master was important, especially at a time like this. Rytsar had to make it clear that he was not a lesser man for offering an apology, something he rarely did.

Rather than a lengthy explanation, Rytsar spoke directly to the issue. "I have been out of my mind with worry after receiving your message, and then I find *radost moya* in your arms. It was too much."

"It was a simple misunderstanding," Tono replied, running his hand over his injured jaw for emphasis.

To show the man he harbored no hard feelings, Rytsar slapped him on the back. "*Radost moya* explained everything to me."

"Where is she?" Tono asked, suddenly looking concerned.

"She was distraught about you, so I came here to apologize."

"What! You left her alone?"

Rytsar sensed Nosaka's rising alarm and said smugly, "She is with her husband, as it should be."

"Didn't she tell you what happened with Sir Davis's half-sister, Lilly?"

A feeling of misgiving washed over Rytsar, but he did his utmost to keep a calm expression, answering only with a "*Nyet.*"

Grabbing his keys, Tono insisted, "We have to go—now. I'll explain why on the way."

Rytsar kept his cool demeanor, assuring the man, "Do not fear, my men are watching over her."

Nosaka was far more intuitive than Rytsar realized. He turned on Rytsar, eying him suspiciously. "Why would you do that?"

Rytsar could not share the truth, but he gave a partial answer that he trusted would pass Nosaka's intense scrutiny. "I trust no one."

The Asian Dom continued to stare at him after hearing Rytsar's blunt answer. Finally, Nosaka shook his head and stated, "It must be a lonely world you live in."

"It is the only one I know."

Rytsar could barely contain his rage when Nosaka shared on the drive back that Brie and the babe had been drugged by Lilly with the intent of kidnapping Brie. He'd beaten the interior of the car to release his fury toward the witch.

No one was allowed to hurt *radost moya* or the baby! Least of all Thane's *suka* of a sister!

Taking a deep breath, Rytsar reined in his fury and apologized to Nosaka. "I am sorry if I damaged the car. I…am very angry right now. But why in the hell is this woman not locked up?"

"The police haven't been able to apprehend her."

"Are they idiots?"

Tono shook his head, explaining, "Durov, this woman is every bit as intelligent as Sir Davis. She has bested us all, and Brie is the one who has paid the price each and every time."

"Well, no more!"

Rytsar could barely contain his fury when they approached the hospital doors and he was stopped by security. He was in no mood to be toyed with and demanded, "What is this?"

Nosaka rested his hand on Rytsar's shoulder. "Violence is not tolerated in this environment. Let me speak with the staff and see what I can do."

Rytsar stood at the entrance and waited, incensed that he was being shut out when it was obvious *he* was the only one who could protect Brie and the babe.

He stood at the entrance, his arms crossed, as he stared down the security guards. There was a sense of satisfaction when they shifted on their feet and glanced at each other. They knew they'd stand no chance against him if he let loose on their sorry asses.

The minutes dragged by slowly.

It was only due to his incredible self-restraint that he had the fortitude not to betray how very close to the edge he was. When he finally saw Nosaka and Brie come through the doors, he snarled, "What took you so long?"

Brie's smile momentarily eased the boiling venom in his heart. "It took some convincing to help them understand you are not a menace to society."

I am not the problem, he thought.

Nosaka added, "They've agreed to allow you into the facility but, should there be a similar outburst, they will call the police."

Rytsar could not waste energy placating the demands of little men and warned, "I won't react unless I am provoked."

"I need you with me," Brie pleaded, her eyes communicating her pain and desperation.

Her simple plea broke through his fiery rage and he vowed to her, "I won't leave your side, *radost moya*."

Rytsar held her in his protective embrace. Whatever

it took, he would find Lilly and make her pay for what she'd done not only to Brie but to Thane. There would be extra vengeance added for drugging Brie and threatening the life of *moye solntse*.

Where others had failed, he would succeed. He was a man without limits and would do whatever it took to make sure that beast of a woman paid for the hell she had caused his friends.

Brie went up to the ICU to say good-bye to her husband before leaving with Rytsar to see Tono Nosaka off. The sooner the man was gone, the sooner Rytsar could put his plans into action.

Both men stood at the entrance of the hospital room watching over Brie as she spoke to Thane privately.

"She's still fragile, Durov. Be gentle with her," Tono warned.

"I will honor my brother in my care of *radost moya*," Rytsar assured him.

"Yes, that is exactly what I did."

Although Rytsar appreciated that the Kinbaku Master had been there for Brie, it was time for him to move on. In no uncertain terms he told Nosaka, "I am his brother."

His thoughts drifted to Brad Anderson and the man's deliberate decision *not* to contact him, and he added, "I still need to even things up with that traitor. I will give him a handshake of thanks—with my fist."

"Who?"

"Anderson."

"You do realize he did everything possible to protect Brie."

Rytsar snorted angrily. "No, he did not, or I would have been here."

"Save your energies for other things," Tono advised.

Rytsar smiled cruelly. "Do you mean that beast of a sibling? She will be sorry she ever touched *radost moya*. When I find her, she will *not* forget my lesson."

"Don't forget Lilly is pregnant, Durov," Nosaka warned unnecessarily.

Rytsar growled. "Rest assured, I do not punish the innocent."

Once Brie had finished her good-byes, she joined them and asked, "Would you like some time alone with him, Rytsar?"

The weight of Thane's life-and-death struggle weighed heavily on his heart and he had to clear his throat before answering. "Yes."

Rytsar didn't approach Thane until after the two left the room.

"*Moy droog…*" He pulled up a chair and lowered the railing. Taking Thane's hand, he clasped it firmly in both of his.

Rytsar didn't say anything at first, pressing Thane's hand against his forehead. "We have been through too much, you and me. It cannot end here."

He looked up momentarily at the heartrate monitor, watching the steady beat. "You must do whatever it takes to return from the abyss. In turn, I promise to eliminate Lilly as a threat." He nodded several times as if he could hear Thane's response. "I know, I know… I give you my word I will not harm the child she carries—but I will have my vengeance. She *must* be made to pay."

The tears started as he reflected on how much he had lost. "It all started with Tatianna…the only reason I came to the US." Her death had forced him to leave the country of his birth to seek out a future outside the motherland that did not involve memories of what might have been.

The prestigious American university he attended provided him with the shock of a new culture and the intellectual stimulation of challenging subjects. He hadn't considered the possibility of companionship until he'd met Thane.

"I couldn't believe what a nerd you were when we first met, comrade. I had no idea then how extraordinary you were." He shook his head, chuckling through his tears. "You have an insanely quick mind—always have. Hell, when I think of the scrapes I got us into and you got us out of…" He looked up at Thane and stated solemnly, "Let's face it, I was the best damn thing that could have happened to you."

Rytsar looked down at Thane's limp hand clasped in his. "And yes, you were definitely the best thing for me." He was silent for a moment. "Only you could have helped me deal with the grief of Tatianna's death. I would have remained in denial, but you understood the devastation of losing a loved one to suicide—and the immense guilt suffered afterward. Oh God, the damage it does to the soul… Yet you willingly exposed your open wounds to me." He squeezed Thane's hand. "That rare gift saved my life, *moy droog*. I've never forgotten it."

Rytsar let go of his hand and stood up, needing to gain supremacy over his emotions. He wiped away the tears but looked down at Thane in sorrow. "I knew we were truly brothers when I realized that your mother matched the cruelty of my father. We shared a similar story, you and I. We had endured more than most at our age, yet still lived to fight another day.

"But then Samantha happened." Rytsar started pacing. "I went from complete elation when I met her to utter decimation. The pain and humiliation she caused that night scarred me." He turned to face Thane, adding, "But I never blamed you, brother. You couldn't have known what she would do—the vile assault…"

Rytsar stood at the foot of the bed, staring hard at Thane. "In my mind, she was no different than the maggots who hurt Tatianna. I would have killed her for what she'd done if you hadn't prevented me from strangling her at the party. I resented you for it then— but I thank you now."

He began pacing again. "I was forced to return to my motherland because I still longed to kill her. As much as I hated leaving you behind, *moy droog*, I was grateful to reunite with my beloved mother after those years apart. How cruelly vindictive Fate is that I returned just in time to witness her death."

Rytsar stopped pacing and closed his eyes. The memory of it tried to ram its way through, but he wouldn't allow it. Shaking the vision from his mind, he sat down next to Thane.

"You proved the strength of our brotherhood when you forsook your own future to travel overseas and hunt me down when I'd failed to check in." Rytsar chuckled sadly. "Seeing your face again was the last thing I expected. I was on the brink of oblivion, but you pulled me out of the darkness. I don't know how you did it, *moy droog*, but you did."

Truth be told, if it hadn't been for Thane, there would have been another suicide—his.

"Having already walked me through the grief of losing Tatianna, you were the only one who could navigate me through the violent murder of my sweet *Mamulya*."

He looked down at Thane with tears in his eyes. "You are an incredible force, comrade. As I was intent on dying. The day I lost my mother, I lost my entire family."

The circumstances surrounding his mother's death had forced Rytsar to sever all ties with his father and, subsequently, his brothers. He spat angrily, thinking back on the reason for her death. "All because my father was a fucking coward. The very same man who took pride in making the whole world fear him." He looked out the window, snarling, "My only desire was to end it all and hopefully drag the sniveling bastard with me to Hell."

Rytsar sighed. "But no. You wouldn't allow me the satisfaction. Instead, you forced me to see a future with purpose and coaxed me forward on a new path until I eventually stepped into it on my own. It took months—I have no clue how you put up with my stubborn Russian ass—but your dedication paid off."

He took Thane's hand and clasped it again in gratitude. "I could see beyond the hate and despair that filled my world. I am eternally grateful for your influence."

Rytsar leaned in close to Thane's ear. "But here's the thing. The darkness has returned, and the one man who could save me isn't here. I need you, brother."

Thane made no move, and there was no change on the heartrate monitor.

Rytsar shook his head. "I wish you had not kept silent about this threat from Lilly. And I would be angry with you, comrade, if I hadn't done the same to you. Once again, our lives seem to mimic each other."

He closed his eyes for a moment, and his mind immediately traveled back to that horrific moment. Unable to stop it and with his heart pounding in his chest, Rytsar relived the pain as the vision took over. His mother was smiling down at him from the upper-story window, waving good-bye to her son just as the dark shadow approached behind her...

"I'm sorry to disturb you, sir, but I need to check Mr. Davis's vitals and take a quick blood sample."

Rytsar looked up at the nurse, the rawness of his pain unveiled for a fraction of a second. He heard her sharp intake of breath as she responded to it. Rather than backing away in fear, she surprised him by reaching out to touch his shoulder.

He instantly retreated into himself and looked the other way.

"Mr. Davis *is* recovering, although it seems like a slow process. There is no reason to lose hope."

"Can you promise me he'll recover?" he asked in a gruff voice, turning back to her.

The nurse smiled sadly. "No."

Rytsar nodded curtly, glancing at her name badge. "Proceed, Nurse Abby."

Standing up, he put the railing back up and placed

the chair in its original spot. "And thank you for your honesty."

He walked out of the ICU and addressed his men. "Titov is in charge of security at the beach house. Both of you will remain here to watch over Sir Davis. I do not want his wife to grow suspicious of your vigilance, so disarm her by smiling whenever she walks past. If she asks how you are, give her a pleasant answer. I want her to think you are here for Mr. Davis as a friendly courtesy of mine."

They nodded, their expressions somber. Rytsar pointed his finger at them. "*Don't* fail to smile."

He headed down in the elevator to meet up with Brie and Tono outside the hospital entrance. He felt a twinge of jealousy when he saw them together and paused for a moment.

It was apparent that the bond Nosaka shared with Brie remained strong. It was not common for Rytsar—this jealousy—and it left him feeling unsettled.

That was another reason to get rid of the Asian Dom as soon as possible.

Then he would have to deal with his old college friend—Brad Anderson.

Rytsar watched the private jet take off, feeling a sense of relief as he wrapped his arm around Brie's waist. "It's good Nosaka can go back to his woman."

She nodded, smiling to herself. "I am pleased about

that."

He guided her into the car and instructed his driver to take them to the beach house.

"Wait. Why aren't we headed back to the apartment?"

"You're joining me at my house while I'm here," he explained. "Titov will be at your disposal whenever you need to leave it."

Brie did not look happy about the arrangement. "Rytsar, while I deeply appreciate the offer, I prefer to stay at the high-rise."

"I am sorry, *radost moya*. That is not an option."

"Why?" she pressed.

"Unlike Master Anderson and Tono Nosaka, I am not willing to put you in harm's way, even if it upsets you."

He saw the flash of defiance in her eyes.

Rytsar raised an eyebrow in response to her willfulness.

She frowned. "But what about my things? And poor Shadow?"

"Your clothes are being packed and brought to my beach house as we speak, but what is this shadow you speak of?"

"He's a black cat."

Rytsar looked at her strangely. "When did Thane become a cat person?"

"Shadow was charged to me when his owner passed away unexpectedly. Sir hasn't met him yet."

Rytsar laughed. "I will be interested to see if this Shadow remains a part of your household after Thane awakens and returns home."

Brie gave him a devastated look.

"Do not fret, *radost moya*. If you wish to have the creature join us at the beach house, I will have it brought along with your things."

"But you don't understand," she insisted. "He doesn't let just anyone to touch him. Besides me, Tono has been the only one."

Rytsar scoffed. "All this concern over a cat? I'm certain my men can handle it."

"I'm not so sure," Brie said, shaking her head. "I think I'd better go back and get him myself. I don't want anyone to get hurt."

He kissed the top of her head. "You amuse me. You do realize my men have dealt with the *bratva*."

Brie still remained unconvinced.

Rytsar smiled confidently. "If they have any trouble, I will retrieve the animal myself. I have something much more important in mind for you."

She lowered her gaze, obviously still struggling with being displaced against her will.

"The upside to submitting to my demand is that I guarantee I will apprehend Lilly."

She looked up with a spark of hope in her eyes. "Really, Rytsar?"

"There are spies everywhere, *radost moya*. It will not be difficult."

The hopeful expression quickly turned to one of concern. "You should know she carries a child."

"I have already been informed that she is pregnant, and I would never cause harm to a child."

"What exactly are you planning to do with Lilly?" Brie whispered in a hushed tone.

Rather than answer her, Rytsar unbuckled her seat belt and pulled her over to him before buckling her back in. He laid her head against his shoulder. "You and the baby are safe with me."

Rytsar was gratified when he felt her relax against him. He smiled, content in the knowledge Lilly would pay for the harm she had done.

Confronting the Traitor

Knowing how long Brie had lived with the pain, fear, and uncertainty of Thane's accident, Rytsar wanted to become her refuge. The first thing he did when they arrived at the beach house was to remind her of their past.

He walked her straight into his bedroom and told her to strip.

She looked at him questioningly but slowly undressed.

He bound her to the middle beam, just as he had the night he'd won her for the auction. However, this time he only blindfolded her.

Rytsar walked to the large windows that made up the west side of the room and opened them so the ocean breeze and the sound of the waves could fill the room. He then returned to her and whispered gruffly, "Your task is simply to reconnect with yourself."

He left the room, shutting the door behind him.

"Titov, remain here and watch over her. I have a pressing engagement with an old college buddy." He smashed his fist hard into his hand and headed toward the door.

Titov stopped him, handing over an envelope, stating, "It's from Russia."

Rytsar took it from him and walked out the door. He glanced over the message on his way to Anderson's place. Folding it back up, he stuffed it in the breast pocket of his jacket. He had to keep his mind focused and not allow it to wander. If his trusted informants were correct, there was little time left. Without a second to lose, the first thing on his agenda was taking care of Anderson's mismanagement of the situation.

He hadn't warned the man he was coming. Anderson didn't deserve the courtesy.

Two of Rytsar's guards followed him to the door to ensure he would not be disturbed during their "discussion".

Pounding hard on the door, Rytsar yelled, "Open up now, you cretin!"

He continued to pound until the door opened. Rytsar was shocked to see a pretty little redhead answering the door. "Can I help you?"

Rytsar frowned and demanded, "Is Anderson here?"

"Why, yes he is. He was just getting…" She blushed, not finishing her sentence as Brad hobbled to the door on his crutches, his shirt only half tucked.

Brad grinned warmly at him. "When the hell did you get in, Durov?"

Rytsar didn't even bother to respond. He pushed hard against Brad's chest, slamming him against the wall inside his home.

Anderson dropped his crutches, thrown off by the unexpected attack, and sputtered, "What the fuck, man?"

The redhead screamed at Rytsar, pounding on his back with her tiny fists.

Rytsar ignored her, getting right up into Brad's face.

"You never called me," he hissed, his muscles twitching, aching to release the rage that was boiling to the surface.

"Look, that's not my fault. Someone else was in charge of it."

"Let him go," the girl demanded behind him. "Brad has a broken leg, for heck's sake!"

"And I'm about to break the other one," Rytsar growled in answer.

"What kind of monster are you?!"

"I am not the monster here." He turned his attention back to Brad. "Have we not been friends since college? Why did you betray me like that?"

Brad pushed against him, but got nowhere. "Look, my only concern was making sure Brie was safe. Nothing else matters. Not you, not me, or anyone else."

"But you called in Nosaka," Rytsar shot back.

"Nosaka was able to give her something no one else could."

"What? I'd really like to know."

"Peace."

Rytsar snarled, unimpressed.

"I don't think you understand how bad off she was," Brad insisted.

Rytsar's blood pressure shot straight back up, and he pushed harder against Brad's chest. "And the reason I don't is because… You. Never. Called."

"Look, man, I'll tell you whatever you want to know but I'm having trouble breathing here."

Rytsar let up, but only slightly, unsatisfied by the answers he'd received so far.

"Who is this man?" the redhead cried.

Brad glanced over at her and gave her a charming smile. "This here is my old college friend, Rytsar Durov."

He turned to Rytsar and introduced her. "Durov, this is my girlfriend, Shey Allen."

Keeping one hand pressed against Brad's chest, Rytsar held out the other to shake hers. "I heartily wish we were meeting under better circumstances."

She shook his hand tentatively, while she looked at Brad in concern.

"Don't mind Durov. He wears his heart on his sleeve and right now he's been put through the wringer."

Brad spoke directly to Rytsar. "I know it's a shock. I still haven't gotten over hearing the news of Thane's plane crash. I can't reconcile the condition he's in right now." He paused for a moment to collect his emotions.

"Even if you believed I'd been informed about the crash, why is it you never bothered to pick up the phone to see how I was handling the news?" Rytsar accused. "Why was that, *friend?*"

Brad nodded. "You're right, you're right… I failed as a friend, but I was in a spiral myself. Don't you get that? I was barely hanging on by a thread. And here I was, in a new position as head of the Submissive Training Center but needing to keep Brie safe from that maniac of a stepsister." His voice faltered slightly when he admitted, "I struggled to cope."

Shey came up to Rytsar and started gently tugging on his arm, trying to release Brad from his unforgiving hold.

Rytsar admired the bravery of the girl. He pushed away from Brad out of respect for her—but was still furious at him.

Shey rushed to Brad's side, checking him over and asking if he was okay.

"Of course, darlin'," Brad answered, casually wrapping an arm around her. He looked at Rytsar and smiled. "This was just a simple greeting among friends. Right, Durov?"

Rytsar huffed. "I do not forgive you."

Brad's infectious laughter filled the hallway. "Nor would I expect you to. But why don't you and I sit and have a drink in Thane's honor?"

"I will drink to Thane, but not because I forgive you."

"Yes, you've made that abundantly clear."

Shey picked up the crutches and handed them back to Brad. As the two men moved into the living room, he asked, "Darlin', do you mind filling up two glasses, one with whiskey and the other with vodka?"

"Ice for Mr. Durov?" she asked him.

"No, we both like it neat."

She glanced over at Rytsar. "Do you promise not to attack my boyfriend while I'm getting your drink?"

"*Nyet.*"

Anderson laughed. "No need to worry, Shey. He and I go *way* back."

The redhead accepted his assurance and winked at Brad as she left to pour the drinks.

Rytsar noticed Brad studying him closely. "What?"

"I'm just wondering how long it took you to get here after you heard what happened."

"I left immediately for the airport, didn't bother packing any bags."

Brad nodded, seemingly impressed by his answer. "Well, misunderstandings aside, I'm glad you're here now. I'm sure Tono could use the extra hand."

"I sent him home."

"What?" Brad looked stunned and confused. "He's already gone?"

"It was the first thing I did after apologizing for punching him."

Brad's jaw dropped. "You hit the guy?"

"I thought he had it coming." His expression became more menacing when he added, "But in reality it was you that fist was meant for."

Shey walked in with their drinks just in time to hear his threat. "Oh no, Brad has done nothing to incur your wrath, Mr. Durov. Ask anyone. He has busted his butt to keep the Center running while looking out for Mrs. Davis and myself. He does not deserve your violence."

Rytsar did not smile when he took the drink from her. He enjoyed the rabbit-like fear he saw in her eyes, but he also admired the girl for her obvious loyalty toward the traitor.

So Brad had finally bagged himself a woman…

Rytsar noticed her jump when he spoke. "Go get another glass, and bring the bottle of vodka back with you."

She looked annoyed, but went back to fetch the two items without complaint.

"Are you a two-fisted drinker, Mr. Durov?" she asked when she returned, handing over the glass and bottle.

The girl had spunk, Rytsar thought. Brad had done well for himself.

He poured the vodka into the empty glass, filling it nearly to the brim before topping his own off, unsatisfied with the amount she'd poured him.

He handed one of the glasses to her, stating, "If we are drinking in honor of Thane, you should not be left out."

Turning to Brad, Rytsar raised his glass. "To Thane, a man above men."

"Hear, hear!" Brad replied, the three of them holding up their drinks.

Rytsar downed the fiery liquid and slammed the glass down on the table to pour himself another. He watched in amusement while Shey took tiny sips of her vodka.

"You will have to train her better. This girl wouldn't last a second in Russia." Rytsar held up his glass to Shey. "A toast to you. It appears my college friend has finally met his match." He downed the drink and grinned at her afterward. "You have no idea what you have gotten yourself into, Shey Allen."

Shey blushed and then giggled, shaking her head, unsure how to respond to him.

"Drink up," he commanded, giving Brad a wink as he downed a third drink.

When the redhead continued to nurse her first drink, Rytsar addressed her in a somber tone, "I will be deeply insulted if you do not finish that shot."

"This isn't a shot, Mr. Durov," she protested. "It's a whole glass of vodka."

"Take it from a Russian, that *is* a shot and you are falling behind. To not drink what was poured you is considered a grave insult amongst my people."

Shey looked at her drink nervously but tipped the glass back and took several gulps before the fiery bite of the liquor got to be too much for her. She sputtered and wiped her mouth sheepishly afterward.

Rytsar returned his attention back to Brad and said reproachfully, "Lilly came close to kidnapping Brie." The simmering anger in his belly started to boil when he thought about how close it'd been. Rytsar spat in disgust. "*That* would never have happened if I'd been here."

Brad nodded, his expression pained and full of guilt. "I failed to grasp how truly dangerous Lilly is."

Rytsar glared at him. "She will be dealt with now."

When Brad started to protest, he raised his hand. "I know, I know, the beast is pregnant. The fetus will be spared."

Brad settled back on the sofa. "I can say I'm actually relieved. No one has been able to stop her. But you? You are a true force to be reckoned with."

"No one hurts *radost moya*," Rytsar stated. "And you? You still deserve a sock in the jaw for putting her in danger. You're lucky Nosaka acted as your whipping boy." Rytsar grunted, adding, "He took it like a man, by the way."

Brad held his hands up in surrender. "Look, I've learned my lesson. Either talk to Durov first or an innocent man will be made to pay."

"It is no laughing matter."

Brad nodded, the smile leaving his face. "I was wrong not to reach out to you."

Rytsar eyed him suspiciously.

Brad stuck his hand out to shake Rytsar's. "Seriously. It won't happen again."

When Rytsar finally took the outstretched hand, Brad shook it vigorously.

Shey gulped the last of her vodka and exclaimed proudly, "I'm done!"

Rytsar knew the warming effects of the vodka were now flowing through her veins. "Good. I will leave unoffended."

He stood up and started toward the door with Shey following close behind him. He stopped her when he noticed her unsteady gait. "I appreciate the courtesy, but I can see myself out."

Rytsar put his hands on her shoulders and turned her around to face Brad. "Go back to your man and enjoy the effects of the vodka."

He left Anderson's still feeling edgy.

Not having the opportunity to release his pent-up anger by breaking bones meant he still had to carry it. Rytsar desperately needed a sadistic session of play, but knew there was no time for such things.

Having promised Brie he would get the damn cat, he had his driver take him to Thane's apartment. His men had done a good job getting Brie's things together, and two large suitcases sat at the front entrance with a list of everything inside.

However, the cat was not among the requested items.

He looked at the two men who were standing at attention with their hands behind their backs. "What's this? I specifically said the cat was coming."

The men shifted uncomfortably.

"What? You're telling me it escaped?"

"Not exactly," said the shorter of the two, revealing his arms to Rytsar. They were covered in angry scratches. Rytsar frowned and asked the other, "You too?"

He only nodded as he showed off similarly slashed arms.

Rytsar shook his head. "One cat did this to my men? My men who have fought trained killers?"

They lowered their eyes to the ground in answer.

"Fine, I will take care of it myself. Where is the beast?"

"In the back bedroom."

"Get out of my sight," he told them in disgust.

His men grabbed the suitcases before leaving the apartment. Rytsar started down the hallway, shaking his head and muttering to himself, "If you want something done right, you have to do it yourself."

Rytsar entered Thane's bedroom and was hit by a moment of grief. The place seemed vacant and depressing, only reminding him of what had been lost. He snarled at himself, having no time to get sentimental.

"Hey, *kot*, I've seen what you did to my men. There's no reason to fight me. I'm only here to deliver you to your mistress."

He looked around the room and saw no sign of life. Getting on his hands and knees, Rytsar checked under the bed. He saw two glowing eyes staring back at him. They narrowed as he met the cat's gaze and a low growl emanated from under the bed.

"I don't have the time or patience for this. Come now," Rytsar said, sweeping his hand as he grabbed for the cat.

Claws and fangs met his attempt, and he instinctually pulled his arm out from under the bed. Rytsar looked down at the scratches, which were already started to itch. He growled angrily. "Oh yeah? Two can play at that game."

Throwing the mattress off the bed, Rytsar lunged for the huge black cat. It waited for him, not moving until it had a clear shot and attached itself to his chest. Rytsar roared as he flung the creature from him, panting heavily.

"You are the devil," Rytsar hissed. "Why she wants you, I'll never know but you're coming with me whether you like it or not. My will over yours, devil *kot.*"

Rytsar ripped a blanket from the disheveled bed. "What I lack in claws I make up for in shrewdness."

It took a half hour to subdue the creature, but subdue him Rytsar did. Holding up the howling bundle in the blanket, he shouted, "Who's the victor now?"

Rytsar caught his sweaty, frazzled reflection in the mirror and had to laugh at himself. All this commotion for a damn feline? It was ridiculous! However, he had the menacing animal in his clutches and would be able to return it to *radost moya* unharmed.

Now he, on the other hand, had not been not so lucky. The cat had gotten in several vicious attacks—but no matter. The spirited tussle had helped relieve some of his pent-up angst and he felt revived from it.

Patting the squirming bundle, he exclaimed, "I cannot be defeated, no matter my foe."

One of his men cleared his throat, and Rytsar glanced up to see him at the entrance of the bedroom. How long he had been standing there Rytsar could only guess.

"May I take it for you?"

Rytsar nodded, handing over the moving bundle. "I will need this room put back together."

"Of course."

As they were walking down the hallway, Rytsar asked, "Are you impressed that I actually caught the damn beast?"

"*Da*. Boris and I tried unsuccessfully for hours."

"That is why *I* am the boss, and you are not," Rytsar said, smacking him on the back. The cat let out a long yowl in answer.

"I do not understand pet people, do you?"

"*Nyet,*" Rytsar answered, spitting on the ground. "I do not believe my comrade will be pleased when he finds out he's now a cat owner."

Blood Bond

W hile they headed back to the beach house, Rytsar reflected on Anderson's claim that Brie had been through far more than he knew. He had no doubt it was true, and suspected Brie was in need of an escape—and, frankly, so was he.

Rytsar called Titov and gave him new orders. Afterward, he sat back in the seat and watched downtown LA pass by as they headed toward the coast. The traffic was unbearable, so he closed his eyes, thinking back to that very first moment when he'd met Brie.

The auction room was full, but he was escorted to the front along with Titov, his "interpreter" for the evening. Rytsar smiled when he saw the girl on stage getting blindfolded after being reprimanded for glancing at a Dom out in the audience during the auction.

While Rytsar understood the reason for the correction, he strongly disliked the person who'd delivered it.

He watched with interest as the girl took her punishment with grace and actually stood a little straighter, oozing a high level of confidence once the blindfold was secured. It was impressive considering how new she was.

Thane had already shared with Rytsar his admiration of the girl, but Rytsar had chalked it up to a case of his American friend's overactive libido.

It pleased him to find that Miss Bennett was adept at playing out the role of the virgin captive she'd written about in her fantasy journal. She made the scene well worth the effort he'd put into planning it.

Even now, his cock throbbed when he thought back to that moment when he'd sunk his shaft into her tight ass as tears fell from her eyes.

He was the first to persuade her into doing something she hadn't been prepared to do. That she'd submitted and embraced the spirit of the scene he'd carefully crafted, endeared her to him.

That singular moment of her surrender remained etched in his mind years later. He'd felt her sheer terror when she'd clawed the floor trying to escape his clutches...

Rytsar had taken her warrior fantasy seriously and wanted it to be fully realized for Brie. So, without reservation, he'd pulled her back and gently hushed her, wiping away her tears before he positioned his cock against her ass again.

The girl, still new to submission, made the conscious decision to accept his desire—and her own—allowing her fantasy warrior to claim not only her body but her will.

It was at that moment he knew Thane had chosen well.

Rytsar shook his head, staring out the window at the sea of cars stopped in traffic. He adjusted his hardening cock in his slacks.

He looked forward to spending the evening with Brie and sharing those memories together. He'd planned a brief escape into their past, adding a ritual that would cement his vow of protection now.

With his comrade lying unconscious in the hospital, it was his duty and honor to fill that role.

He spoke to Titov before rejoining Brie. "How is she?"

"I heard quiet sobbing and checked on her. Mrs. Davis must have heard me enter because she suddenly stopped and has remained quiet ever since."

Rytsar nodded, stating confidently, "She needed this release."

He strode into the bedroom, making no attempt to be quiet.

"Rytsar?" Brie called out.

"*Da, radost moya*," he answered. "It is I, your Russian knight."

As he approached, Rytsar noticed her blindfold was soaked with tears, but Brie wore a peaceful expression on her lips.

Brie said aloud, in a wistful voice, "The ocean is eternal, Rytsar. The sound of the waves acts as an audible reminder that time never stops. The tragedies and triumphs of this world are washed away in their unrelenting movement."

"A profound musing."

She lowered her head and smiled. "The bound isolation, combined with the sound of the waves, has had a significant impact."

"Good. Those moments are needed when chaos reigns, and you are correct, *radost moya*. Nothing in this world is permanent. Not you, not me, or the land we stand on now."

She lifted her head, raising her chin a little. "Except true love. The vibrations of love never dissipate."

Rytsar shook his head and chuckled, tugging on a lock of her hair. "Still such an innocent."

She frowned slightly.

Rytsar was captured by the look of her, bound and blindfolded, yet still standing up to him. "Respectfully, Rytsar, you should not be so quick to dismiss my belief. I see in you the love of your mother and the love you hold for Tatianna. Love like that does not die. It makes you stronger. You still feed on it when you have need," she declared gently. "Am I wrong?"

Cradling her cheek, Rytsar answered, "No, *radost moya*. You are not wrong, but more than their love sustains me."

He placed his hand on her stomach. "My brotherhood with Thane, you, and the babe. You three give me strength I can no longer survive without."

Rytsar untied her wet blindfold and let it fall to the floor. Wiping her cheeks, he leaned down and kissed her gently on the lips.

When he pulled away, she smiled until a look of concern came over her. "Oh no...what happened to you? Just look at your poor arms."

He looked down at the numerous scratches and shrugged. "It's nothing."

Brie shook her head begged, "Please untie me."

Rytsar undid her bonds and as soon as she was loose, Brie grabbed his arms to look at them more closely. "We need to take care of those. The last thing you need is an infection."

"Don't make such a fuss, woman," Rytsar protested when she headed to the bathroom to get supplies.

Brie hurried back out with a washcloth and a container of rubbing alcohol.

"I told you it's not necessary to make a fuss," he grumbled.

Brie looked guilty as she poured the alcohol onto the cloth. "I take it by looking at your arms that Shadow didn't come quietly."

Rytsar grunted. "Like you, he is stubborn."

Brie bit her lip as she started to clean the deep scratches. "I'm sorry it burns."

Laughing, he told her, "I'm a Russian. I do not cry over scratches."

"Still, he did a real number on you." She looked worried when she asked, "You didn't hurt him, did you?"

"*Nyet.* Your little pet made it here safe and sound."

"Can I see him?"

"Not yet. I have other plans for us first."

Brie nodded and went back to tending his wounds. The simple act reminded him of his mother, so he acquiesced even though it was not needed.

As she worked, Rytsar noted a change come over Brie as tears started to fall. "We are connected—the three of us. I still remember how it felt when you left us in China after Sir's mother died. It was as if a part of me was ripped away when you left."

"*Da*, I felt it too," he answered gruffly.

The loss then only echoed the extreme loss the two of them felt now. Rytsar hushed her when the tears did not stop.

"I have a surprise for you, *radost moya*."

She looked up and attempted a smile. "A surprise?"

Rytsar didn't say more as he dried her tears before taking the cloth from her hand and laying it on the table. Snapping his fingers to alert Titov, he smiled at Brie while they waited.

Titov entered the room holding a large box, which he handed directly to her.

"Change into these and nothing else," Rytsar commanded. "I will meet you outside."

He left her with a slight grin on his face, knowing her curiosity had been piqued.

Rytsar headed out the front doors and whistled in admiration when he saw the stallion standing proudly before him. Voin was still as magnificent as the day he'd first laid eyes on the fine beast. He was a stunning equine, worthy of such a name.

Hearing a giggle behind him, Rytsar turned to see

Brie wrapped up in a short white coat and furry boots that showed off her bare legs.

"Makes me think of our last encounter in Russia," he growled huskily as he pulled her to him.

"I look dressed for Russia, not the California beach," she teased.

"The evening air is cool, *radost moya*. We must keep you and the baby warm." In a gliding motion, he jumped onto the horse and held out his hand to her. Brie grasped it and broke out into a peal of laughter as he easily hoisted her onto the horse in front of him.

Already he could see his plan was working. The enthusiastic young woman he'd met at the auction was reflected in her actions and voice now as Brie stroked the mane of the stallion.

"Rytsar, I never did ask you his name."

"*Voin.*"

She repeated the word before asking, "It's a fine, strong-sounding name, but what does it mean exactly?"

"Berserker."

Brie tilted her head questioningly, apparently unfamiliar with the term.

"Mighty warrior," he stated.

"Ah…" She patted the beast's neck. "Then it's the perfect name for the fantasy he helped carry out."

Rytsar nuzzled Brie's ear before biting down and saying huskily, "It was a memorable fantasy, *radost moya*, written by a woman with great imagination and inspired desires."

He wrapped his arm around her before nudging the horse with his heels to start them on their journey down the coastline.

Brie leaned against his chest and sighed contently. "This is nice, Rytsar."

He smiled to himself as the sun slowly disappeared behind the horizon and the waves lapped against the stallion's legs.

"*Da,* I have often thought back on that evening with you."

She tilted her head back to look up at him. "Really? With all the erotic things you have done as a sadist?"

"It was a tender moment—your surrender when I claimed your ass."

She trembled. "I was in awe and fear of you that night. Just thinking about it gives me pleasant goosebumps."

"You still feel that way?" he growled, biting lightly on her ear.

"You definitely hold a unique power over me," she admitted. "I'm both frightened and totally captivated by you."

"And you should be." Rytsar clicked his tongue and Voin sped up, the horse falling into a gliding lope. He appreciated the feel of the ocean breeze, along with the whipping action of Brie's hair against his cheek. Yes, this was a welcomed and needed escape.

Rytsar headed down the beach until he came up to the fire that had been prepared for them. Brie squealed in delight as they approached and she saw the blanket laid out beside the fire ring.

"Our own private fire on the beach. Just like old times!"

"A stolen moment for you, me, and the babe." He slid off the horse and offered his hand, helping her to gently dismount. Brie fell into his arms and gazed into his eyes.

Time seemed to stop.

He felt the same connection he'd had with Brie at the Russian cabin. She was easy to love and she was a part of Thane. It was easy to find solace in her arms.

Only she could truly relate to the profound shock he'd felt upon learning of Thane's accident. The uncertainty of knowing whether his comrade would recover and if he would be the same man only made it that much worse.

There was always the chance his brother would not survive—which he would not acknowledge aloud—but it was the reason he wanted to bring her here tonight and perform the same ritual he had with Thane years ago.

He was doing it as much for himself as he was for her.

Rytsar led her to the fire and gestured to the blanket as he commanded her to kneel. Rytsar sat beside her cross-legged. Taking her small hands in his, he told her, "*Radost moya*, you know the deep friendship I share with your husband."

"Of course."

"You also know the love and respect I hold for you."

She nodded, smiling at him, her eyes luminous in the firelight.

"It extends to the wee babe you carry."

Brie grinned, caressing her stomach. "I know how dearly you love *moye solntse.*"

"Because of those three things, I wish to perform the ritual of blood with you."

She suddenly looked frightened and pulled away. "What are you talking about?"

"Thane and I became blood brothers in college." He showed Brie the old scar on his left wrist. "It speaks to our level of commitment to one another."

"I have always admired your brotherhood."

"Tonight, I wish to make a similar vow to you."

Her eyes widened, the flames of the fire dancing wildly in their reflection.

"I promise you my fidelity, protection, and comradeship. It is the exact same promise I made to Thane."

Her eyes filled with tears. "I am truly honored."

Rytsar pulled out a mean-looking blade and presented it to her. The metal glinted in the firelight, highlighting its sharp edge.

"Is this the knife you used with Sir?"

"It is. You and I will mix blood as a symbol of my vow. I do not do this to take my comrade's place, but to stand beside him, ensuring you and the babe will want for nothing."

Brie looked down at the fierce blade with fear in her eyes, but took a deep breath and nodded.

"So you are willing, *radost moya*?"

Brie pushed back the sleeve of her coat to bare her left arm to him, gazing into his eyes. Although frightened, she understood the meaning and significance behind his offer. "Sir told me the day we found out I was pregnant that I was to trust you if anything ever happened. It's the reason we named you as our baby's godfather."

"What? Why didn't he tell me? I specifically asked the night I learned I was going to be her *dyadya*."

Brie smiled. "Sir said he didn't want it going to your head."

Rytsar huffed in frustration. "He was in a jesting mood that night, wasn't he?"

Brie leaned her head against his shoulder. "Sir couldn't wait to tell you about the baby, Rytsar, and he was the one who bought the vodka so we could tell you in a way only you would understand."

Rytsar felt his throat catch and had to wait a moment before he spoke. "I have that picture you sent as my screensaver on all my devices. I feel joy every time I see that bottle with the line through it."

"Sir would be glad to know that."

They both stared at the flames in silence. Speaking of that momentous night only high-lighted the significance of their loss now. Despite Rytsar's stated optimism, he still feared he would not see his comrade again.

Laying the knife down on the blanket, he took out a white strand of cotton from his pocket, putting it on the blanket beside the blade. Rytsar then undid his tie and unbuttoned his shirt, shedding his clothes and laying both to the side.

Brie's gaze never left his as Rytsar prepared himself.

"We do not want to bloody your pretty white coat," he explained as he slowly unzipped it and helped her out of the jacket, laying it beside his own clothing. It left her naked except for her furry boots.

Rytsar saw the goosebumps rise on her skin. He was

certain it was caused by a combination of fear and the cool night air. It also had a pleasing effect on her nipples.

Brie instinctively wrapped her arms around herself, but he commanded, "Hold out your left arm."

She sucked in her breath, but dutifully held out her arm to him. Rytsar noticed her tremble slightly and smiled to himself. *Radost moya*—his beautiful non-masochist.

Positioning her wrist over the sand, he told her nonchalantly, "No reason for us to bleed on the blanket."

Brie let out a barely audible whimper but smiled at him hesitantly.

Rytsar picked up the blade and held it before her. "Tonight you and I unite together with blood. As we mix our life forces, we bind ourselves to one another. This bond speaks to my undying loyalty to you and cannot be broken."

Having made his vow, he placed the blade just above his old scar and punctured his skin, dragging it slowly across. Brie gasped as blood started to flow from the new wound.

Rytsar gave a low grunt of pleasure.

Taking her hand, he grasped it firmly as he positioned the blade against her delicate wrist. He held it there for several seconds, wanting to prolong this important moment for her.

Brie needed time to reflect on the bond being formed tonight.

"Tell me when you are ready."

She looked up at him with a surprised expression. She'd expected only to submit to this ritual, but Rytsar demanded her participation.

Gazing into his eyes, Brie made her vow to him. "I pledge my undying loyalty to you, second only to my Master." She looked down at her wrist pinned by the blade and did not hesitate. "Now."

He pushed the tip of the sharp edge, breaking the skin. To her credit, Brie made no sound although her eyes became wide as he cut her skin.

Rytsar thrust the bloody knife into the sand after the incision was made and picked up the strip of white cotton. He bit onto one end as he pressed his bloody wrist against hers and wrapped them tightly together.

Crimson soaked through the first layers of the white fabric as he continued to bind them together. Once bound, he finished with a simple knot.

"Lie with me," he commanded, pulling Brie down onto the blanket and pressing her body against him. He stared out at the dark ocean, the constant crashing of the waves just beyond the light adding to the eternal element of their act.

Brie pressed against him.

"I am a berserker, *radost moya,*" he confessed solemnly. "I am a fierce protector. *No* one can hurt you now."

"I believe you."

He kissed the top of her head. "As far as *moye solntse,* she will want for nothing."

Brie looked into his eyes. "Please don't spoil our child. I don't want a sweet little brat on my hands."

He crushed her to him and laughed. "I make no promises."

Brie settled against him and he noticed her smile

contentedly as she turned back to the flames.

"I can imagine it already," he whispered gruffly. "You holding the wee babe as Thane and I smile down at her."

"Or him," she corrected quietly.

"Or him," he replied for her benefit even though he knew it was a girl.

"Yes…I can see that too," she replied wistfully. "It *will* happen."

"Of course it will," he stated, but his heart was still troubled. "*Moye solntse* will know the depth of her *dyadya's* love."

"I'm glad." Brie did not correct him this time on the sex of the baby. She looked down at the white cloth that bound them together and asked, "Should I consider you my blood brother now, Rytsar?"

He snorted. "*Nyet.* I am not your brother." He pulled on her hair, tilting her head back to plant a firm kiss on her lips. He looked deep into her eyes, overcome with a sense of profound responsibility. "My role is to step in for Thane when he cannot."

Brie nodded, a poignant smile on her lips as she accepted his words.

Rytsar squeezed her tighter. It felt as if she, like he, had left a part of her soul with Thane at the hospital. Until his comrade was with them in body as well as spirit, nothing would feel whole or right.

He covered them both with the blanket to protect them from the cold night air. He stared into her honey-colored eyes as he thought back to the first conversation he'd had with Thane about the girl lying beside him now.

"Hey, Durov, glad I caught you before you headed out for the day. I have a favor to ask."

"Shoot, *moy droog*," Rytsar answered, short on time but curious about his comrade's request.

"We have a new submissive at The Center who intrigues me. Would you be willing to come to our first auction and bid for her?"

Thane kept his distance from students—it was a rule he never broke. Rytsar's interest was stirred. "What makes this particular sub so special?"

"I can't put my finger on it. It's one reason I want you to come. I need your honest opinion of her."

Rytsar was left momentarily speechless. Thane was unusually adept at reading people, especially new subs. That he was seeking Rytsar's opinion meant the girl was having an unwelcomed effect on him.

That could actually be a good thing… However, not just any girl would do. Thane needed a woman worthy of his talents and strong enough to withstand the challenges he presented as a partner.

It was only right that Rytsar was being called in, but sadly he had no time for a jaunt off to America. "You know normally I would say yes, *moy droog,* but—"

"This is not an idle request."

His answer had serious undertones, grabbing Rytsar's attention. "Go on."

"I have broken protocol and had sexual contact with the girl after class hours."

"I don't believe it."

"I would chalk my behavior up to an uncommon level of lust but for one thing. When I finished, I did not feel the elation of conquest. Instead, I felt…"

"What?"

"Exposed."

His confession struck Rytsar. He had only felt that way once—a long time ago—with Tatianna. No further urging was necessary. "I'll come. What is the sub's name?"

"Miss Bennett. I want you to make her first auction memorable."

"Do not fear, *moy droog*. I will make it an evening she won't forget."

"She's not like the submissives you normally play with, my friend. Be gentle with her."

Rytsar grunted in amusement. "This girl, she has already stolen your heart."

"Don't be absurd."

Thane's immediate denial was telling. The reality that his comrade had fallen for a woman was sobering to Rytsar. There was a reason to hope.

"It would be my honor to assess the girl, but if I find her unworthy, I will not mince my words."

"I'm counting on it, old friend. I need clarity and you are the only one I trust to give it."

Rytsar was determined to put this girl through the paces. If she didn't prove a worthy match, it was better Thane knew now before he become more emotionally invested.

"I'm afraid there's one thing that may change your

mind about coming," Thane cautioned.

"Nothing could keep me away, I swear it."

"Samantha will be on the panel."

Rytsar growled. To be in the same room with that woman would require more control than he could muster. "You are asking too much of me, *moy droog*."

"I wouldn't ask if I didn't need you here."

Rytsar glanced down at the scar on his wrist. They had a bond that was stronger than family. The fact Thane was asking this of him only highlighted the gravity of the situation.

"Send me a copy of Miss Bennett's fantasy journal."

"Good, I'll see you soon then."

Rytsar chuckled reluctantly. "Apparently so."

Thane paused for a moment. "Thank you, brother."

"No need to thank me. I get to tease and fuck a sexy American. In truth, I should be thanking you."

"There's just one more thing."

"*Da?*"

"She's not for going back to Russia with you."

Rytsar burst out laughing. "No worries, *moy droog*. Trust me, I am not interested in your plaything." After he got off the phone, Rytsar shook his head. It was clear that his comrade was in deep over his head.

Tormented Past

L ooking down at the woman in his arms, Rytsar smiled to himself. Thane's request that day had ended up changing the course of both their lives. Brie not only brought balance to his comrade's life, but to his own.

"Rytsar," she said gently.

"Yes, *radost moya*?"

"I'm glad you're here."

"I was supposed to be here all along." He glanced at their joined wrists and asked her, "Are you ready to be unbound?"

She nodded.

Rytsar helped her into a sitting position as the blanket fell away, leaving them exposed to the chill of the air. He noted again the pleasing effect the ocean breeze had on her pert breasts. Brie was truly a beauty, and with the blush of motherhood she'd become irresistible to him.

He began unwrapping the cloth, now soaked with their blood. He picked up his bottle of vodka and splashed the alcohol on her wounds to clean and sanitize them.

Brie sucked in her breath and he grinned. Yes, it stung, but it was the good kind of pain.

"Now, we each carry the mark that symbolizes our blood bond."

Brie lightly traced a line just above her wound, which was still trickling a small amount of blood.

Rytsar fished out gauze and bandaged up her wrist before taking care of his own. He then wrapped her back in the white coat and zipped it up, patting her on the head like a child. He felt a profound love for her and picked up the bottle of vodka to celebrate it.

Pressing it to her lips, he commanded, "Drink."

"What about the baby?"

"Just one sip."

Brie nodded and swallowed the fiery liquid, smiling at him afterward as tears pricked her eyes.

He grunted in gratification, taking several long swigs for himself before setting the bottle down and putting his clothes back on.

Rytsar helped Brie onto the stallion, then jumped up behind her.

"This night will be forever etched in my mind," Brie commented softly, lying back against his chest.

He felt a deep sense of satisfaction. Already he had started the process of setting things right.

When they reached the beach house, he helped her down and handed the reins over to one of his men who was waiting outside. Unbeknownst to Brie, they had been guarded by his men the entire time. He would take no chances with her.

Once inside, Rytsar told her to check on the cat while he headed to the shower to steal a few moments for himself. He could feel the tick of the clock with each passing second he spent with Brie.

His instincts were telling him there was very little time.

Rytsar came to bed after toweling off. Brie was already sitting on it, petting the black creature. One look at Rytsar, and the feline jumped from Brie's lap and made a beeline for the door. She stood up and smiled. "Shadow thought you were taking him away from me. I think that's why he fought so hard." Looking at Rytsar's shredded arms, she added, "It wasn't personal."

Rytsar shrugged. "I hold no grudge against it, but the animal has no reason to run now."

"I'm afraid that's the way he is around most people, regardless of the circumstances."

"Except Nosaka," Rytsar stated.

"So far—yes."

"Well, it doesn't matter. As long as you are happy, it can spend its days hiding like a coward."

Brie smiled, unconsciously glancing at Rytsar's naked frame. A pink blush colored her cheeks as she looked away.

It had been a long time since they'd been together intimately. He was certain the poor girl had not experienced release since Thane's accident. He knew what she needed and would speak to his comrade about it in the morning. It was not healthy for Brie to lock away the passion of her soul, especially with a sex life that had been as intense and prolific as theirs.

"Do you normally wear that to bed?" he asked, looking at the long white nightgown covering her feminine curves.

"Not with Sir, of course, but I have been lately." She looked down at the simple gown. "It was something I used to wear in college."

Rytsar eyed the unflattering nightgown but said nothing as he threw back the covers and crawled into bed, slapping the mattress, inviting her to join him.

Brie lay down beside him and rested her head on his pillow, staring at him silently.

"What are you thinking, *radost moya?*"

She shook her head slightly. "I don't think you want to know."

Raising an eyebrow, he told her, "Try me."

Brie took a deep breath before answering, alerting him to her discomfort. He hoped it was a filthy desire he could use in the future with her.

"I was thinking back on our conversation about your mother in Russia. I'd like to ask what happened to her—now that you and I are bonded by blood and all."

Rytsar stared at her, saying nothing. Bringing up his mother required a complete reversal of thought. Speaking about his mother's death only brought him great sadness, and with the current situation, it seemed unwise to delve down into that dark hole with Brie.

Still…would he ever have the chance to share that part of himself with her if he didn't do it now?

Closing his eyes, he allowed the horrifying memories of his mother's last moments to come flooding back and his heart broke all over again.

"My mother was thrilled to see me when I unexpectedly came back from the States. I assumed by the lines on her face that she'd been worried about my well-being, although she had never confronted me on it."

Rytsar looked at Brie. "I never told her what happened between Samantha and me, but somehow I think she knew—a mother's instinct. When Mama met me at the airport, she held on to me, refusing to let go."

A tear traveled down his cheek. "I loved her, *radost moya*. I am not ashamed to say that my mother held my heart in her gentle hands."

Brie hugged him, trying to keep her own tears back.

He looked down at her sweet face and smiled sadly. "How I wish you two could have met. She never had the chance to meet *moy droog*…"

Brie cocked her head. "I had no idea Sir never met her."

Rytsar let out a long, tortured sigh. "*Mamulya* only lived a few days after my return to Moscow."

Shaking her head in disbelief, Brie snuggled closer to him. "What happened to her?" she asked in the barest of whispers.

"She was murdered. It was a hit, *radost moya.*"

Brie stared at him, too stunned to speak.

"My mother's kind soul was snuffed out by a cold-hearted killer."

"But I thought your family didn't deal with the *bratva.*"

"We don't."

"It wasn't a mistake, was it?" she asked in horror.

"Her death was payment."

"For what?"

"A gambling debt."

Brie looked confused. "But you don't gamble."

"It was not my debt." The vision of his mother's death played out before him as he spoke. "It is burned in my memory and is something I must fight off every day."

"I can't believe you were there when it happened," she whispered, tears filling her eyes.

Rytsar pressed his forehead against hers. "I must live with the fact that I...couldn't save her."

"Oh Rytsar..."

He pulled away from Brie, forcing himself to voice aloud the vision in his head. "That night started off deceptively sweet. My mother had laughed so much that night when I'd shared the most humorous stories involving Thane, Brad, and me. She countered my college tales with her favorite pranks I had played as a young boy." He smiled to himself. "It was a rare and precious moment."

Brie gently kissed his forehead, smiling sadly.

"I left her just before nine, intent on spending a night out with my old gang." He stopped for a moment, hardly able to voice the memory he had kept buried for so long. "I was jumping into my car when I happened to look up at the window and saw her waving at me."

Rytsar felt his world crashing in and had to clear his throat, pushing himself to continue. "I saw the outline of the assassin as he approached her from behind, his actions swift as he unceremoniously slit my mother's throat. The man let her fall and looked out the window at me. I raced to the door, but I had locked it on my way out and had to fumble for the keys.

"I knew even as I rushed up the stairs I was too late to save her. *Mamulya* lay in a pool of blood as her heart steadily pumped out the last of her life. The assassin was gone, and I had the choice to chase after him or stay with my mother during her final moments."

He paused, his voice choked with emotion. "I chose to stay."

Brie silently wept the tears he could not.

"As my beautiful mother lay gasping in my arms, she wore a surprised expression on her face. She tried to speak to me, but only gurgled on the copious amount of blood as I watched the light slowly ebb from her soulful eyes."

A chilling cry escaped his lips at the memory of her final breath.

Brie pressed his head against her breasts, letting out a strangled cry of her own. The two became silent as the echoes of that loss played out.

"Anton," she whispered, "I am so sorry you carry this burden."

He lifted his head and looked at Brie strangely. It was uncanny how much she'd sounded like his mother just then.

Rytsar shook his head to clear it. "Although an assassin killed her, I knew who the real murderer was and I raced to confront my father. I found the fucking bastard at a poker table."

He roared in anger thinking about his father, the blood pounding in his head as red filled his brain. Rytsar was physically shaking, and had to push himself away from Brie, uncertain if he could control the hostility he felt.

He explained as he made his way to the door, "If I say any more, *radost moya*, I will have to punch something. Neither it nor I will survive without something breaking."

Rytsar disappeared into his study to let the darkness in his soul pass. He watched with approval as the cat scrambled out of the room as if the hounds of hell were chasing him. In Rytsar's current state, he was capable of anything.

Sadly, his blind rage was the only notable characteristic his father had passed down to his son—the ability to become a berserker and annihilate everything in his path.

The night of his mother's death, Rytsar had gone into full berserker mode, creating a path of destruction in his wake. It would have been the perfect irony if his father had died that same night at the hands of his son. But the patriarch of the Kozlov family had denied Rytsar the satisfaction, having spared Rytsar's life that night. The mercy shown had been out of sincere respect for him, but Rytsar had suffered for it ever since.

It took several hours before Rytsar felt calm enough to return to bed. The dark rage he still harbored had no place here, not with *radost moya* to look after now.

Rytsar wandered into the kitchen to fill up a large glass of water. He opened the fridge and glanced inside it for something savory. He spied some pickles and went to grab them when his eyes drifted over to the cooked bacon. Snagging it up too, he sat down near the cat, who was crouched under the far sofa thinking itself hidden.

While Rytsar munched on the pickles, he held out the bacon to the cat.

"Who can resist bacon?" he stated, wiggling the treat to entice the beast.

It stared at him warily, making no move toward the meat.

After several minutes, feeling foolish for even attempting to befriend the animal, Rytsar placed the bacon on the end table. "Suit yourself. Your loss."

He finished another pickle and gulped down the cold water before heading back to his bed. To her credit, Brie had remained in the bed, respecting his need for solitude.

Rytsar had assumed she'd be asleep and tried to be quiet, but when he walked inside the bedroom, he found her kneeling beside the bed, patiently waiting for his return.

He was touched.

"You should be resting."

Brie looked at him with compassion. "I cannot sleep when I know you are suffering."

Rytsar felt a sadistic need to test her. "The only thing that would help is a good session with my 'nines."

The look of terror in Brie's eyes made him smile inwardly.

"I…"

In a demanding tone, he asked her, "*Radost moya,* are you serious in your desire to ease my pain or not?"

He felt a surge of inner excitement seeing her shiver.

"Stand facing the pole if you are in earnest."

Rytsar was extremely curious what Brie would do,

knowing well her fear of his cat o' nines.

Brie didn't move a muscle for several moments, then nodded to him and gracefully made her way to the pole. She rested her body against it, willingly exposing her back to him.

Her willingness to sacrifice herself for his well-being moved Rytsar far more than she could know.

Determined to continue his wicked test, Rytsar walked over to Brie and grabbed the material of her nightgown, ripping it in two with his bare hands.

She cried out at the violence of the action but stayed in place.

Rytsar ran his fingers over her bare skin before picking up his 'nines. He started warming up his muscles.

While the sound of the tails slashing the air excited him, he knew it frightened her and watched with pleasure as the muscles of her back tensed in anticipation of their cruel caress.

It was hard not to hold back his mirth when he told her, "I am not in a gentle mood."

Brie let out a soft whimper but remained still. Her dedication to him was truly priceless.

Rytsar let out a low animal growl, followed by the question, "Are you ready to receive my 'nines, *radost moya?*"

Her body said no, but he heard a timid "yes" come from her lips.

"Good."

Approaching her trembling frame, he whispered in her ear, "Your willingness was all that I required."

Brie let out her breath and turned to him, her cheeks

wet with tears. "Are you sure?"

"Yes." Rytsar kissed her on the forehead, stating, "You are an extraordinary soul."

Brie suddenly frowned, understanding she'd been set up. "You, Rytsar Durov, are a wicked, wicked man."

He looked at her in pretend shock. "I would never hurt you unless you begged me to. Even then, I would have to consider the babe you carry." He caressed her stomach tenderly. "Although you are not a masochist, I love that you are irresistibly drawn to my power."

He stared at her lips and leaned in closer. Brie did not move, inviting the advance.

There was a burning need to connect with her after the devastation of the plane crash. It had left a gaping hole so deep that demanded to be filled.

They could be that for each other...

Rytsar stopped short. Rather than kiss her, he wrapped her in his muscular arms and pressed her naked torso against his. He could feel her heart beating rapidly like a scared little rabbit.

"I must rest now. There is much I must accomplish tomorrow."

Brie nodded, stepping back when he let go, the flush of before returning to her cheeks. The mutual longing for connection was easy to read.

"Will you be able to? Rest, I mean," she asked.

He answered by picking Brie up and carrying her to his bed. "Your devotion has eased my dark soul for the time being."

Brie curled up beside him, resting her head against his chest. "I have missed this kind of closeness."

Rytsar grunted in response, grateful that Nosaka had not filled that role while caring for her. The man gained more respect in Rytsar's eyes. Maybe a gift was in order to make up for the sucker punch he'd given the Kinbaku Master.

He would arrange something nice.

"Go to sleep," Rytsar commanded gently as he reached over and turned off the light. He noticed one of his men outside the glass window, walking the perimeter. It gave him a profound sense of peace.

He was a Durov. He didn't just get mad, he got even.

Starting with the beast known as Lilly.

Casting the Net

T he next morning, while Brie was still sleeping, Rytsar slipped out of the bed and put on a robe, heading outside to greet the pale light of a breaking dawn. The ocean waves were unusually big, the sound of them crashing against the shore an excellent cover for the discussion he was about to have with his men.

"Titov, are you positive?"

"*Da*. We know where she is hiding. It's not far."

Rytsar looked at all of his men. "You understand what needs to happen today. It must be seamless."

They nodded in unison.

"Leave nothing behind. Make it as if she never existed. You know the price if you fail."

Again, his men nodded.

"And the man, Reese?" Rytsar asked, turning to Titov again.

"He left the county the day of the incident and is keeping a low profile in the Virgin Islands."

"Then it should be easy enough to silence the maggot," Rytsar snorted.

"Only a matter of a day or two."

"Excellent."

Rytsar reminded his men, "Be mindful the criminal is pregnant. While the woman will be made to suffer, there will be no harm to the child under your watch." He made each of them agree individually.

"I will be heading to the hospital with Titov this morning. Call me once you have secured the captive and I will join you." Rytsar looked at his men and said somberly, "Move with stealth and purpose—succeed where others have failed."

The men pounded their chests three times in unison, physically voicing their commitment.

With Rytsar's plan now set in motion, he would have to share the details with Thane. It mattered little to Rytsar whether Thane remembered the conversation or not. This he was doing for his own peace of mind.

"Go now," he told his men. He watched as they headed out—the thrill of the chase being denied him. No matter; he would soon have his vengeance.

Shedding his robe, Rytsar walked toward the ocean in the buff. He dived into a breaking wave, exhilarated by the rush of cold water. There was nothing like shocking the system when darkness consumed the soul.

Rytsar smiled broadly when he walked out of the water and saw Brie standing on the beach waiting for him. "Would you like to take a dip before we head out, *radost*

moya?" he asked, picking her up in his arms and twirling her about, covering Brie in cold droplets.

She cried out in surprise and then started laughing.

"Is that a yes?" he teased, as he headed toward the water.

She struggled in his arms, pleading, "No, no, no... Please no water sports!"

He chuckled dangerously, remembering fondly his impish joke at the cabin. "I'm sorry, that is not the proper response you were taught at The Center, now is it?"

"Rytsar, don't!" she screamed as he headed into the water, waiting for the right wave. When it rose up before them, he launched her into the air.

He watched with pleasure as she disappeared under the swirling water, only to pop up a few seconds later whimpering, "It's so cold, it's so freakin' cold..."

The waves were strong, and unlike him, Brie could not keep her balance when the next one hit. Down under the icy waves she disappeared again.

Taking pity on her, he grabbed a flailing hand and pulled her to him, cradling her body in his arms as he carried her back to shore and set her down.

He took delight in her chattering teeth and the tiny goosebumps that covered her skin as they walked back to the beach house. "No need to thank me."

"For...what...?" she sputtered.

"For clearing your mind," he said, chuckling to himself.

Titov opened the door as they approached and Rytsar picked her up carried and her to the oversize whirlpool tub already filled with warm water.

He set her down into it, stating, "Wasn't it refreshing?"

Brie looked up at him, her lips blue from the cold and her teeth still chattering. "Nnnnn..o."

She stared at the steam rising around her and purred through her chattering teeth, "It's so nice and warm."

Rytsar stepped into the tub to join her and Brie settled between his legs, leaning her back against his chest. Picking up a bar of soap, he lathered his hands before running them over her body. Had the situation been different, he would have found the encounter more sexual in nature and made advances to ravish her. However, in his current state, he found this moment a welcomed respite from the storm.

Brie must have felt the same because she relaxed against him, letting his hands glide over her body. How long had it been since she had known the intimacy of companionship?

"How are you feeling today, *radost moya*? Really?"

She turned her head and looked at him sadly. "No matter what I'm doing or who I am with, I feel desperately alone without Sir."

Rytsar nodded in understanding, grateful for her candor.

The pleasant sound of trickling water echoed in the large bathroom as he lifted one of her arms up and thoroughly lathered it before rinsing it off.

"Your soul is torn in two," he stated. "I understand."

"Yes... I never understood what a lonely place the world could be."

Her words struck a chord in Rytsar. Most of his adult life he had felt that way. The only time he'd truly felt connected to the world around him was when the three of them came together. Thane was his stable foundation—unmoving and true. And Brie was his heart—open and joyous.

"It is a cruel and lonely place, *radost moya*. However, there is strength in unity."

He carefully washed the length of her other arm before heading for her chest.

"Yes, I agree that there is." Brie added with a sigh, "However, it's not the same without Sir."

"No. It is not."

He put down the soap and wrapped his arms around her. "Thane will join the living again but, until he does, I will act as your foundation."

"Yes, Rytsar," she said with a shy smile.

That smile stirred something in him. As they were drying off, he took the opportunity to caress her body with the towel. He reflected on the softness of her skin, the tautness of her nipples, and the beauty of her womanly curves.

It would be a shame to let this lovely creature wither away with need.

"I have something for you," he stated huskily. Once they were fully dressed, he snapped his fingers and one of his men appeared with a bouquet of flowers, which Rytsar handed to Brie with a slight bow.

"What are these for?" Brie giggled in delight.

"I know you like them."

She grinned as she lowered her nose to take in the

scent of the colorful arrangement, not knowing they were silk flowers. She glanced up, looking at him oddly.

"Do you know why I didn't get you real ones?"

Brie shook her head, looking confused.

"I want you to know that my bond will not wilt or die over time."

Brie crushed herself against him. "Oh Rytsar…"

Rytsar wanted to make the most of the time he had with Brie, and decided to share a secret obsession he and Titov shared. They took a slight detour before heading to the hospital. Brie's interest became piqued when Titov suddenly parked the vehicle and jumped out, running to the opposite side of the street.

"What is he doing?"

Rytsar only smiled when Titov disappeared into a tiny donut shop and returned with a small white box.

"Have you ever had one?" Rytsar asked her.

"Donuts? Sure. Who hasn't?"

"These are not *donuts*," he scoffed. "These are a culinary adventure for the palate." His mouth began watering at the thought of biting into one of the unusual creations.

Titov opened the car door and handed Rytsar the box before getting back into the vehicle himself.

Rytsar stared down at the box, hesitating to open it. He looked at Brie and said gravely, "I'm serious, *radost moya*, you will be forever changed with one bite. It will become a craving you won't be able to satisfy."

She laughed out loud. "You do realize you sound like a vampire right now."

He only smiled, taking his time to open the box for dramatic effect, revealing four distinctive creations inside.

"This one," he stated, pointing to a rich wine-colored one, "this is *mine*."

"Okay," she replied with a shrug. "But it looks like a simple berry donut to me."

"Ah, but it isn't. This is Blueberry Bourbon and Basil."

Rytsar could see he had her attention now.

Taking a napkin, Rytsar picked up the powdered donut and handed it over the back of the seat to Titov. "His favorite is the Orange Olive Oil."

Titov grunted in agreement. "I enjoy the texture of this particular donut and the citrus powder it's dusted in." He kept one hand on the wheel as he took a huge bite.

Rytsar looked down at the other two donuts. "I was unsure which you would prefer so I chose two." Pointing to the chocolate donut smothered in chocolate ganache, he said with a smirk, "I know that you sometimes prefer it dark so I got you the Hot Chocolate." He then pointed to the white one covered in melted sugar with a small squeezable vial of liquor syrup on top. "In case you were feeling a little more Caucasian today, you also have the Creme Brûlée."

Brie stared at both donuts hungrily and, without skipping a beat, picked up one in each hand. "I like it both ways," she announced, first taking a bite of the dark chocolate and then biting into the sugary crunch of the brûlée.

She closed her eyes with a happy smile and purred.

Rytsar picked up the tiny vial of Cointreau. "You greedy little thing, let me follow that with a squirt of tangy liquid."

Brie quickly swallowed before she opened her mouth for him. Rytsar squeezed the orange-flavored liquor into her mouth in short pulses, making her giggle as the tiny bursts landed on her tongue.

"I never knew donuts could be so sexual," she said, wiping an errant drop of syrup from her bottom lip and swiping it over his lips with her finger.

Rytsar winked at her as he licked it from his lips. He glanced at Titov through the reflection of the rearview mirror.

Titov chuckled, taking the last bite of his donut and unceremoniously licking the powder from his fingers.

"We are decidedly an uncouth threesome," Rytsar asserted, finally taking a bite of his favorite donut. He closed his eyes to fully savor the bourbon glaze, and was surprised when he felt his donut move in his hand. He opened his eyes to find Brie taking a bite.

Rytsar growled like an angry dog protecting its food. "Keep those sexy lips away from my donut."

"I'm sorry, Rytsar. I just had to take a little taste. It looks so delicious." Brie licked her berry-glazed lips, adding enthusiastically, "And it *so* is!"

"You have two of your own," he reminded her harshly.

Brie looked genuinely remorseful and held up her chocolate donut. "Would you like to lick my big black one? It's so thick I can barely wrap my lips around it."

Rytsar had to keep from laughing and chose to snarl instead. "I'm not licking that."

Brie glanced down at his crotch and smiled innocently. "That's what she said."

Both men burst out laughing, filling the car with their masculine mirth.

Rytsar was shocked to find Brad leaning on his crutches by the ICU doors when they arrived at the hospital. He resented the intrusion, and realized he still couldn't forgive the man.

Brad made a point to greet Brie first, smiling as he transferred a crutch to his other hand to give her a tight hug.

You're only making it worse for yourself, Rytsar thought bitterly.

Brad let her go and held out his hand to Rytsar. "Look, I've thought about what you said yesterday, and I wanted to come here to apologize formally."

Rytsar stared at his hand with disdain, not making a move to shake it.

Not taking no for an answer, Brad grasped his hand and shook it vigorously. "You were right. I was not a good friend to you. You deserved better from your old college mate."

Rytsar's frown deepened.

Brad laughed uncomfortably. "What can I do to make it up to you?"

"I cannot forgive so easily."

"No, Rytsar, please don't say that," Brie begged. "Master Anderson was good to me and made sure my baby got the nutrition she needed when I was too distraught to eat."

Rytsar snarled. "While I appreciate you looking out for the welfare of the babe, I cannot so easily forgive the wrong committed against me."

Brad shook his head, looking at a loss.

"Well, I for one am so glad to see you," Brie told him, giving Brad another hug. She placed the crutch back in his hand and suggested they all sit down.

"How has Cayenne been doing? I miss that little orange tabby."

Brad's smile quickly turned into a scowl. "My poor, poor baby…"

"On no, what's happened to her?" Brie cried.

"She's having…" he spat the next word out in revulsion, "…babies."

Brie clapped her hands together, crying out happily, "Kittens are wonderful news!"

"No, young Brie, they are not. Your beast of a cat defiled Cayenne. She's still just a kitten herself."

"Apparently not," Rytsar interjected.

Brad glared at him.

"No, no…I'm sure he made sweet, romantic love to her," Brie insisted.

Brad huffed angrily. "You must know nothing about

domestic cats." He ran his fingers through his hair in frustration, growling under his breath. "I knew he was trouble the moment I saw the black bastard."

Ignoring his sour mood, Brie exclaimed joyfully, "You're going to have a house overflowing with tiny kittens!"

"Really? Must you add salt to the wound?" Brad complained.

Rytsar actually found his discomfort entertaining. "Tell me, does this Shadow creature hate you?"

Brad glanced at the scratches on Rytsar's arms and answered, "Not as much as he appears to despise you."

Rytsar punched his fist into his palm. "You are wrong. I just had to show it who was boss."

Brad gave him a sarcastic smile. "That may work on people, but animals are different."

"I beg to differ. But no matter, it's not my pet who's been violated," Rytsar replied with a smirk.

Brad instantly tensed again. Rytsar would enjoy getting mileage out of this unexpected turn of events.

"Well, at least you two are talking again," Brie cooed. "That's worth celebrating and I know it would make Sir happy."

The two men stared at each other, the mention of Thane making everything feel as childish as it really was. "Fine," Rytsar grumbled. "I…" he had to force the word out, "*forgive*."

Brad nodded, a relieved smile on his lips. "I'm glad to hear it. Life's too short to hold grudges."

"I do not agree," Rytsar countered, "but you and I are square."

"That's all I wanted to hear." He gave Brie one last hug before standing back up with his crutches. "I'll let you go to your husband now because I'm sure he's anxious to see you." His hand grazed the bandage on her wrist as he let go of her hand, and he chided, "You need to be more careful, young Brie."

He nodded to Rytsar. "You watch out for her." As he was leaving, however, his eyes landed on the bandage around Rytsar's own wrist and he frowned, glancing back at Brie's.

Rytsar met his troubled gaze. "You have no reason for concern. She is completely safe with me."

"It's not her *safety* I'm concerned about," Brad answered.

Brie broke in. "Master Anderson, you have absolutely nothing to worry about. Rytsar has only Sir's and my best interests at heart."

Brad eyed Rytsar. "Still, I think you and I should have a chat."

"Do not go looking for trouble where there is none," Rytsar warned.

Brad turned his attention back on Brie. "My door is always open, young Brie. Don't let this stupid leg prevent you from calling if you need me—for anything."

Rytsar stood up, trying hard to control his anger. He leaned in close, stating in a low voice, "I would *never* do anything to dishonor my brother. Don't even go there. The fact you would even question it is insulting."

Brad glanced down at his wrist and raised an eyebrow. "Guess you're going to have to explain *that* to me."

"Why don't we discuss it over drinks sometime—like old college buddies," Rytsar quipped.

"Let's," Brad said drolly.

He tipped an imaginary hat to Brie before turning to leave.

"Give Shey my best," Brie called out. "Oh, and give little mama Cayenne an extra squeeze from me!"

Brad grumbled under his breath on his way to the elevator.

Rytsar watched him go with a tinge of regret. Despite Brad's offensive lack of trust, it was good they had reconciled. Who knew if he would be given another chance?

While Brie spoke to Thane, Rytsar took a seat to watch their interaction. Even though it was one-sided, she somehow made Thane a part of the conversation with her comments and facial expressions, as if she could hear him through the silence.

Whether it was foolish to do so or not, her love for Thane was obvious and was comforting for him to witness.

Brie pulled out her computer and plugged in her headphones. "I have some serious googling to do. You can talk privately with Sir if you like." She slipped on the headphones and the faint sound of dubstep could be heard as she bounced to the deep bass while surfing on her computer.

Rytsar took the opportunity to tell Thane his elaborate plans for Lilly. He noted a slight increase in the rhythm of Thane's heartbeat, although nothing else of significance changed. Rytsar was certain what he had laid out met with Thane's approval.

He was about to broach another topic when he noticed the strange expression on Brie's face.

Rytsar tapped her shoulder and she blushed as she slipped her headphones off. "I never knew…"

"Knew what?"

"That it is like that for cats." She looked up at Rytsar with wide eyes. "Something just came to me and I've got to write it down. Pardon me." Brie put her headphones back on and began furiously clicking her keys as if the words couldn't pour out fast enough.

Rytsar watched her, fascinated by the passionate look in her eyes as she typed.

"Your beautiful wife is suffering from lack of release, *moy droog.* I know you can't see it, but it's quite apparent to me."

A short time later, Brie ripped off her headphones again, her eyes shining with lustful excitement. "Can I read you what I just wrote? I totally understand why Master Anderson is upset, but I'm certain it wasn't that way for Shadow and Cayenne. This," she said, pointing to her screen, "is how I imagine it went down."

"Please do, *radost moya,*" Rytsar said with a smirk. "The two of us would enjoy hearing your take on it."

Brie smiled as she glanced back at the screen. Her voice suddenly took on a sultry tone as she weaved an erotic spell with her words. "Shadow looked down at Cayenne lying on the floor, noting her alluring scent. She was a female in heat.

"Shadow knew from experience that there was no denying a female in this state. The instinct to mate was so strong that she would offer herself continuously until seed had been planted.

"But he also knew this was her first time in season. Everything was new and unfamiliar to her.

"Cayenne meowed seductively, prostrating herself on the ground and rolling her hips side to side. She didn't know yet that the act would hurt. His shaft was barbed, created specifically to scratch her inside to stimulate ovulation whenever they coupled.

"'You do not know what you are asking,' he said, jumping down from the bed to join her.

"'Please,' she begged. 'I'm aching inside. I *need* you...'

"'I understand your need, but it will be painful. There's no way around it.'

"'Then make it hurt,' she cried passionately. 'I want you to hurt me.'

"Shadow took in her female scent. Just the smell of her was enough to make his shaft stiff. Even if he wanted to resist her feline advances, nature wouldn't permit it. Once a female was in season, she would be relentless until she was taken multiple times.

"He circled around her slowly, his whole body responding to her inviting mews and the way she stuck her ass in the air, moving her tail to the side so he could see her willingness.

"*Very well.*

"Like she, he was an animal of instinct, and everything in him wanted to hold Cayenne down and claim her.

"He started by licking Cayenne on the back of her

neck. The area he would soon be biting as he shoved his shaft into her.

"She rubbed her cheek against him in response, the heat of her need consuming them both. She meowed again, low and deep. The kind of meow that stimulated his more primal instincts.

"Shadow moved down to her hind end, which she promptly lifted up to him. He began licking her, knowing he was the first male to do so. She purred passionately, 'Oh, that feels so good. So good…Shadow.'

"He continued licking, drawing out this first time—wanting Cayenne to remember the sensuality of the act to counterbalance the pain that was about to follow.

"'Please, Shadow,' she begged again. 'I *need* you.'

"With permission given, Shadow mounted her, pulling her closer to him with his forepaws and taking the scruff of her neck in his teeth. She instantly flattened herself, clawing at the ground as she raised her hips to him, her body begging to be claimed.

"At that point, all reason left as feline instinct took over. He began the exploratory thrusts, his rigid shaft needing to take her. He bit down harder on her neck, and she meowed lustfully, her whole body primed for this moment. He needed to make kittens with her, his soul cried out for it.

"Shadow continued thrusting, knowing that he was excruciatingly close. He changed angle slightly and his barbed shaft finally slipped inside her. He bit down hard and Cayenne tensed, the pain of his entry causing her temporary shock.

"It was enough time to pump her full of his seed before she cried out. But he didn't let go of her afterward. He kept her in that position once he pulled out and waited, growling seductively as he gave his cock time to recover.

"Cayenne lay still beneath him, softly mewing. It was as if her body knew when his shaft was hard again, because her hips began their dance, edging her sweet heaven closer and closer to his shaft. Opening herself to be claimed again.

"This time, she knew the pain it would cause and yet she still begged for it. 'Hurt me, Shadow. Hurt me so good…'

"He let go of her neck momentarily to get a better hold.

"Biting down caused her to flatten herself again, raising that sexy ass in the air, her body pleading for the release and pain only he could provide.

"Shadow growled hungrily as he began thrusting again, seeking her warmth.

"The two remained in that sexual dance, so close but not quite connecting for several moments. It was with great satisfaction when his hard shaft finally found its home, stabbing her repeatedly with its love.

"She screamed in pain and pleasure as he pumped life into her body.

"It soon became too much for Cayenne and she cried out for him to stop. He instantly released her and backed away.

"Cayenne fell to the floor and began rolling beside him, wiggling contently, looking like a playful kitten. What she did not realize yet was that her instinct to roll had a purpose. The act made sure his sperm traveled deep inside her body so when her eggs released they would be penetrated and fertilized by him.

"After several minutes, Cayenne became still and stared at him in longing and fear.

"'What's wrong?' he asked.

"'It hurt so bad, but I want you again.'

"Shadow smiled to himself, grateful that the two of them were compatible as mates. He had a long week ahead of fucking her whenever she called out, but he couldn't wait to begin round two..."

Brie looked up at Rytsar questioningly when she was done. "So, what do you think?"

"It's perfect. In fact, I think you should print it off and tuck it inside a congratulations card for our good friend—to cheer him up."

"You think so?"

"Yes. In fact, I insist you go down to the hospital gift shop and pick out a card right now so you can send it to him." He held out a twenty to her.

Brie's eyes sparkled as she took the money, giving Sir a quick kiss before heading out of the room.

Rytsar turned back to Thane, shaking his head. "What did I tell you, *moy droog*? Your woman has serious needs. I'm sure you can appreciate the toll it takes on her body when physical release is denied for an extended amount of time. With that in mind, I have made a purchase on your behalf. It arrives tomorrow, just in time for me to speak with the obstetrician at your wife's next appointment. Never fear, comrade. Nothing will touch your woman without the doctor's seal of approval."

He left Brie in the capable hands of Titov after receiving word that Lilly had been successfully delivered. Rytsar spoke to his men before entering the room, congratulating them on their prowess.

"No issues at all?"

Yegor shrugged. "None. It was an easy assignment."

"That is what I expected to hear. Well done." Rytsar shook each of their hands before heading into the room.

He was purposely silent so she would not detect his presence as he stared hard at the enemy. Lilly was a freak of nature, the exact replica of Ruth—down to the thin fingers that ended in blood-red fingernails resembling claws.

He cleared his throat and noticed her jump. Rolling her shoulders back to regain her composure, she turned to face him, clutching her bulging stomach in a vain effort to gain sympathy.

"And you are?" she asked dismissively.

"Your nightmare."

She laughed in disgust. "I very much doubt that."

Rytsar walked toward her, eyeing the woman like the maggot she was. "Your breath is mine."

Lilly mistakenly turned away, stating flippantly, "Spare me your dramatics."

In the blink of an eye, he had his large hand around her throat, squeezing her larynx. As she gasped for air he leaned in and hissed, "Do *not* play games with me, *pizda.*"

Rytsar let go abruptly and watched in satisfaction as she struggled to regain not only her breath, but her balance.

"You are going to tell me everything I want to know."

The look of pure hate Lilly shot his way pleased Rytsar far more than she knew. "Don't you *ever* put your hands on me again!"

"Or what?"

Her nostrils flared as she scowled at him, refusing to speak.

Rytsar snorted with amusement. "Do you not see I can kill you with my bare hands? Your threats mean nothing here."

Lilly tilted her head up with a look of superiority. "What I may lack in brawn, I make up for in intelligence."

His laughter filled the small room. "You were easy enough to apprehend, which makes your level of intelligence highly suspect."

She looked at him with disdain, obviously not used to being put in her place.

Rytsar's eyes narrowed, his hate for her easy to read in his voice. "Do not lie to me or you will suffer greatly."

Lilly lifted her chin a little higher. "Buffoon."

Rytsar's eyes flashed with predatory hunger as a cruel smile played across his lips. "I have no problem hurting you to get what I want."

She rubbed her belly with a smirk on her face. "You don't want to harm this baby. Thane Davis is a very important man and he's not going to like it."

"There are ways to torture a woman that do not inflict damage on the fetus."

Her smiled faltered slightly. "Who are you, *really*?"

Rytsar ignored her, barking his first question instead. "Whose child do you carry?"

Lilly did not hesitate when she answered, "Thane's."

"Are you sure you want to stick with that answer?" he asked menacingly.

"What? Do you plan to kill me unless I say otherwise?"

Rytsar gave her a disarming grin, even though rage filled his heart. "What were you planning to do after you drugged Mrs. Davis?"

Lilly shrugged with seeming disinterest. "I have no idea what you are talking about."

His smile disappeared as he turned and started toward the door.

Rytsar could feel her scornful gaze on his back and smiled to himself. Without warning, he turned and rushed her, pinning Lilly to the wall with one hand wrapped tightly around her scrawny little neck.

He lifted her off the ground and stared into her bulging eyes, wild with fear. "I promise you will look back on this day and wish to God you had told me the truth."

Letting her go, he watched Lilly slump to the floor, her hand clutching her throat as she struggled for breath.

Rytsar walked away from her, his boots echoing loudly as he headed out the door. He slammed the door shut and slid the lock into place, letting the clang of it be the last thing she heard before he left.

He went to his men with instructions.

"First, shave off her hair and cut her nails down to tiny nubs. Oh, and strip her. The *pizda* doesn't deserve the dignity of clothes."

"Is there anything else?" Yegor asked.

"Yes, be sure she gets the proper nutrition. If she refuses to eat, you have my permission to shove it down her throat."

"Understood."

Rytsar smiled. "I will be back in two days. I have a special gift in mind on my return."

He chuckled to himself as he left, plotting the many ways he would make Lilly pay for the harm she had caused his little family—Thane, Brie, and his tiny *moye solntse*.

Heartbeat

Rytsar awoke energized about the day ahead. Not only would he have the honor of attending Brie's appointment, but if the obstetrician agreed, he would be introducing her to blessed release that night.

He could hardly contain himself as he took his morning dive into the ocean. He was definitely seeing his life in a far more positive light. The darkness that had haunted him for so long was beginning to lift. Even if this was only a temporary illusion, he was determined to embrace it fully.

Having the Lilly threat locked and contained only added to his overall feeling of exhilaration. It was a good day to be alive.

When he walked into the bathroom for his warm bath afterward, he found Brie waiting for him.

"While I am not into cold dips in the ocean at dawn, I do enjoy a warm bath with a Russian."

He smiled as he dropped his robe and helped her into the tub. "Today is a most special day, *radost moya*."

Brie settled down in the tub, resting her hands on his

thighs, and leaned back, sighing contentedly. "Yes, it is. Today you get to join me at my appointment and see the ultrasound. I will love not going to the appointment alone."

Rytsar wrapped one arm around her and pressed Brie against him. "It was never meant to be that way, *radost moya*. You will always have at least one of us by your side from this point forward."

Brie laid her head against him and said in a wistful voice, "I feel completely safe."

"Today we will add completely satiated to the list."

Brie turned her head and questioned him with a hint of concern. "What exactly do you have in mind, Rytsar?"

"Trust me," he said as he began to lather both their bodies up.

"But you're a sadist and a wicked-mean prankster."

Rytsar held up his wrist to her without saying another word and went back to work, rubbing his hands all over her slippery body with soap.

Brie settled back against him hesitantly. "Fine, I will trust you."

He chuckled as he splashed her with water.

Rytsar guided Brie into the doctor's office and told her to sit down while he signed her in.

"I'm here on Thane Davis's behalf," he said proudly. "I was told there would be an ultrasound today for Mrs. Davis and just want to confirm."

The receptionist smiled pleasantly as she checked the schedule on her computer. "That's correct. And your name is?"

"Rytsar Durov, a relative of the family's."

The receptionist glanced over at Brie. "It's so tragic what happened to her husband, isn't it?"

"Agreed, which is why it's important I'm here as support until he recovers."

The woman blushed, responding to his natural Russian charm. "Mrs. Davis is certainly lucky to have someone as handsome as you as her support."

Although inappropriate considering the circumstances, Rytsar understood her plight. It was hard to resist the allure of his masculine dominance. He gave her a curt nod and sat down next to Brie.

"You know I'm perfectly capable of signing in myself," Brie chided gently. "It's not like I'm helpless."

"*Radost moya*, it is my pleasure to care for you and the babe."

She wrapped herself around his muscular arm and sighed contentedly. "I'll admit it's nice to be pampered."

Several minutes later, the technician called Brie in, instructing her to change into the hospital gown and lie on the table.

Once the man left, Rytsar helped her out of her clothes and tied the gown securely before sweeping her off her feet to set her on the table himself.

Brie giggled as she lay down on the crinkly paper. "Well, I've never had it done so swoon-worthy before."

Rytsar smiled but once she was settled, he stood still, feet apart, arms crossed, and a stoic expression on his face.

"Aren't you excited to be here?" Brie asked after several minutes had passed in silence.

He glanced down at Brie without moving his head, not wanting her to know just how anxious he was about seeing *moye solntse* for the first time. "I wouldn't miss this for the world."

Brie held out her hand to him and smiled. "I'm touched you feel that way."

When the door opened, Rytsar shook the technician's hand firmly, keeping his tough outer exterior, although his heart had started to race.

The man looked over at Brie. "And who is this?"

"Thane's brother, Rytsar Durov."

The technician turned to him. "It's a pleasure to meet Thane Davis's brother. We're all pulling for him."

Rytsar nodded curtly, not trusting himself to speak.

The technician glanced at Brie, uncertain how to take Rytsar's lack of response. "Well, I suppose we'd better get to it then."

"Agreed," Rytsar stated impatiently, taking Brie's hand as he watched the ultrasound technician lift the gown and spread clear gel on her stomach.

"Today we'll be checking measurements," he explained.

"Will you be checking the sex of the baby as well?" Rytsar wanted to know.

The technician smiled. "No, it's still too early to determine that."

"Ah," Rytsar replied, squeezing Brie's hand a little harder, disappointed Brie would not have confirmed what he knew to be true.

Rytsar watched with interest as the technician glided the instrument over her stomach, revealing globular shapes on the small computer screen.

"Which one is the babe?" Rytsar asked.

The technician traced his finger around a small peanut-shaped glob. "This is the fetus."

Rytsar pulled out his phone. "Do you mind if I take a picture?"

"I'm sorry, Mr. Durov, that's not allowed."

Rytsar grunted and shoved the phone back in his pocket, hiding his disappointment.

"But I'll print a picture when I'm done," the technician offered.

"Good," Rytsar said gruffly, his eyes glued on that image on the screen. He couldn't believe he was actually seeing the tiny babe.

"Now, if I zoom in here, you can see the heart beating."

Rytsar felt his own heart stop for a moment as he watched the little miracle of that magical fluttering movement. He moved in for a closer look and turned to Brie. "We can see her heartbeat, *radost moya!*"

Brie's face was glowing and she giggled joyously. "I know. I can't believe it."

Tears welled up in Rytsar's eyes as he turned back to the screen. He watched in reverent silence as the sonographer recorded all the measurements. When the man was done, he handed Rytsar two copies of the picture.

For the first time since entering the room, Rytsar smiled at him, slapping him hard on the back.

The technician was taken aback and cried out in surprise, then laughed awkwardly. Adjusting his glasses, he turned to Brie and informed her, "Your doctor will be meeting with you in a couple of minutes after he's had a chance to look over the results."

"Is anything wrong?" Rytsar demanded.

"Simply hospital procedure, Mr. Durov," the man assured him.

Rytsar looked at Brie to make sure she had not been upset by the man's words. Instead of worry, he saw the glow of motherly confidence reflected in her eyes.

It gave his own soul peace, and he did not accost the man for more answers.

The technician efficiently cleaned the gel from Brie and started toward the door. Rytsar held up the prints and barked a quick, "Thanks."

For some reason, the technician turned and put his hand to his head in a salute before leaving the room.

"A bit odd, that man," Rytsar complained.

"I think he found you intimidating, Rytsar."

"What? Me?"

"Yes, you. Why did you get all serious on him?"

As Rytsar helped Brie into a sitting position, he told her, "I don't like that he wouldn't allow me to film it, and why couldn't he simply tell us the baby is fine? I don't trust his silence."

Brie placed her hand on his arm and smiled gently. "That's what they did the last time. I remember feeling scared too at that first ultrasound, but the baby was just fine. And we just saw that little heart beating away. There's nothing to worry about."

Rytsar stared down at the little peanut in the picture and nodded. He leaned over to kiss Brie's stomach before whispering, "I see you, *moye solntse*, and you are even more beautiful than I imagined."

There was a knock on the door before the obstetrician stepped in. "Oh, I see we brought a bodyguard with us today."

Brie laughed sweetly. "Yes. This is Thane's brother, Rytsar Durov. Rytsar, this is Dr. Peterman."

"Good to meet you, Mr. Durov," the doctor said, giving him a firm handshake.

Rytsar's first impression of the man was favorable, which was important since he was in charge of both Brie and the babe's care.

"Now, let's get down to business," Dr. Peterman stated, wheeling the stool over and sitting down next to Brie. "Looking at all the measurements, it appears the fetus is smaller than most but completely within normal range."

Rytsar blurted, "I was afraid something was wrong. Tell me, was the babe hurt when she was drugged?"

The doctor held up his hand. "I understand your concern, but everything is checking out normal. There is no reason for worry." He looked at Brie and smiled. "In fact, why don't we listen to the heartbeat? I'm positive it will ease both your minds."

Rytsar took ahold of Brie's hand again and returned to his stoic state as the doctor had her lie down again and he placed another coating of gel on her stomach. With a smaller device, he began sliding the instrument to the left side of her stomach. Seemly out of nowhere, the loud sound of a quickly beating heart filled the small office room.

Rytsar was overwhelmed by that sound of life. He felt no shame when a couple of tears escaped. "She sounds so strong…"

"Now we don't know the sex of the child at this point," the doctor corrected, "but yes, that is a healthy heart rate."

Rytsar glanced at Brie and said nothing.

She nodded in response, both of them lost in the wonder of *moye solntse's* heartbeat.

The doctor was about to remove the device when Rytsar asked him, "Do you mind if I record it for the father?"

Brie's eyes lit up. "Yes, can we please?"

"I see no reason why not," Dr. Peterman answered.

Rytsar hit record and let it run for several minutes before nodding and saying thank you afterward.

While the doctor cleaned off the gel, he told them, "Unless you have any other questions, we're done here for today."

"Actually," Rytsar answered, "I do have a question that I would like to ask privately."

The doctor looked at Brie. "Only if you allow it, Mrs. Davis."

Brie gazed tenderly at Rytsar. "My husband and I trust him completely."

"Very well. Meet me in my office in a few minutes."

The instant the doctor disappeared, Rytsar picked Brie up and twirled her around in the small room. "She is healthy and strong, *radost moya!*"

Brie laughed as he set her gently on the ground.

"I am going to be a *dyadya*."

"You've known that for months now."

"But this is the first time it has felt real."

Brie smiled, leaning her head against him. "Yes, I can understand that."

Rytsar escorted her back to the waiting room before heading into the doctor's office. Dr. Peterman asked him to sit and shut the door so they could talk.

"This may seem strange of me to ask, Doctor, but with Mr. Davis in critical condition and his wife without his company, I was wondering if this device would be safe to use even though she's pregnant." Rytsar handed the man his phone with the Sybian website already cued up.

"Ah…" the doctor said, looking surprised as he examined the sex machine. "I can't say that I am familiar with this particular tool."

"It was created by a scientist with the sole purpose of satisfying women. The level of vibration is controlled by the user and there are different attachments depending on the woman's body type and level of need."

"What kind of attachments?"

Rytsar took the phone back and flipped to that page, showing him. "As you can see, it varies from simple external stimulation, to small internal inserts, and even life-size phalluses. The internal attachments can simply vibrate or move in a circular motion to stimulate the G-spot, or do both at the same time."

"I see."

"Do you think using this would compromise the

health of the baby?"

"Having no experience with the product myself, I cannot recommend it. What I *can* tell you, however, is that normal vibrators are perfectly acceptable as long as they are cleaned thoroughly. Avoiding forceful penetration, especially with rigid devices, is important."

"Of course," Rytsar agreed with a smirk. "No rigid phalluses."

"Dildos," Dr. Peterman amended. "I'm speaking about vibrators."

"That's what I assumed we were talking about."

"Good," Dr. Peterman said, looking uneasy. "It's important for me as her doctor to be clear on this."

"And you were," Rytsar assured him, looking amused.

Dr. Peterman regained his composure and ended their conversation with a professional summary. "Basically, a woman achieving orgasm will not hurt the baby as long as the device used does not stress the mother internally."

"Thank you, Doctor."

Despite his confident stride, Rytsar headed out the door weighed down with concern. The Sybian was well-known for its strong vibration. In fact, many women had to build up to the intensity of the rotating phallus and its heavy vibration to achieve a mind-blowing orgasm.

He'd assumed it was the perfect solution to sex without Thane present, but he was wrong. Now he'd have to switch to Plan B. Well, it couldn't be helped— and who's to say he wouldn't enjoy the change of plans?

Rytsar headed back to the waiting room to find Brie.

"Did you get the answers to your questions, Rytsar?"

"I did. You have a fine doctor there—humorous too. And I'm taking his suggestion under advisement." He wrapped an arm around Brie. "But now it's time to share the heartbeat with your husband."

"Yes! Let's," she agreed enthusiastically.

When they entered Thane's hospital room, Rytsar noted that his comrade's condition hadn't changed from the days before. However, rather than get discouraged by that fact, Brie grinned as she took Rytsar's phone from him and skipped to Thane's bed.

"Sir, we just came back from my latest baby appointment and guess what? Rytsar recorded our baby's heartbeat for you! Here, let me play it."

She placed the phone near his head and set it on speaker so the room filled with the life-affirming sound. Both Rytsar and Brie watched with excitement as Thane's heart rate increased as he listened to the recording of his child.

Brie turned to Rytsar. "He knows! Sir can hear his baby's heartbeat."

Rytsar nodded, too choked up for words. This was proof positive that his brother was cognizant, despite the lifeless stare of his eyes.

"Do you feel it, *moy droog*? Hope is yours to claim."

Rytsar watched with interest as his friend's heart rate continued to increase—so much so that the nurse came in to check on him.

"What's going on here?" Abby asked as she hurried in.

"It's the baby," Brie answered. "Sir is listening to the

baby's heartbeat."

Abby put her hand to her mouth, a look of cautious optimism on her face.

Brie returned her gaze to Thane. "You totally hear it, don't you, Sir? Let that beautiful sound carry you back to me."

Rytsar stayed with Brie beside Thane's bed for the next few hours. Eventually his comrade's heart rate returned to its slow, steady beat and he stopped responding to the recording.

"What happened?" Brie whispered, her tears falling onto the bed. "He was so close. I could feel it."

"He's simply tired. *Moy droog* needs time to rest so he can fight again tomorrow."

Brie buried her head in Rytsar's chest. "It hurts…"

Rytsar held her close, feeling equally devastated. He remained by her side until she could take the silence no more.

"I need to get out of here."

"Why don't we go back to the beach house?"

She stared at Sir for several minutes before nodding. "Every positive change is a step toward recovery, right?"

"Yes," Rytsar affirmed.

Brie gave him back the phone before stroking Thane's cheek. "Rest now, Master. I will keep waiting, but I am impatient for your return." She gave him a soft, lingering kiss before following Rytsar out the door.

Brie was unusually quiet on the ride home. After such a momentous day, it was disturbing for him. "You must keep your spirits up if you want to help your man recover."

She gave him a sideways glance and rested her head against the window, saying nothing.

When Rytsar arrived at the beach house, he asked Titov to set things up in the bedroom while he grabbed a bottle of vodka and a shot glass. He sat down in the big leather armchair and motioned Brie to join him at his feet.

She smiled sadly as she settled down beside him.

"I know you cannot partake with me, so I thought I would stroke your hair while I celebrate meeting *moye solntse.*"

Brie looked up at him with those big doe-like eyes, shivering as his fingers played through her brown curls. She closed her eyes and purred softly, laying her head on his thigh. She shivered again, goosebumps rising on her skin as he made another slow pass. "It feels so good."

Rytsar took a big gulp, embracing the burn of the alcohol. "Ahhh…I couldn't agree more."

They stayed there enjoying each other's quiet company long after Titov returned to let Rytsar know the room had been readied.

The fact was, he enjoyed this quiet moment with Brie. Experiencing the highs and lows of the day had bonded them closer and he wasn't in the mood to rush things. After downing his second glass, however, Rytsar finally gave in to the girl's unspoken needs and helped Brie to her feet.

"Undress in the bedroom and kneel in front of the gift set out for you."

Brie tilted her head. "Gift?"

"Yes, today we are taking a step toward bringing balance back into your life."

He stayed behind to share one more shot with Titov. "Today has affected me deeply." He put his hand on Titov's shoulder. "I am grateful for your service these many years."

Titov scoffed, brushing off his praise. "Phhft... You pay me well."

Rytsar squeezed his shoulder firmly. "I am serious." Pointing to his own eyes, then at Titov, he said, "I observe everything and I reward loyalty. You will be able to retire handsomely if I survive, or..." he added with a shrug, "you will die a terrible death for associating with me."

Titov chuckled. "Such is life."

Rytsar raised the glass to him and grinned. After he downed it, he bit into a salty pickle. The tart flavor burst in his mouth, bringing forth a grunt of pleasure.

"It is good to be magnificently, unapologetically Russian."

"*Da*," Titov chuckled.

Retiring to his room, Rytsar shut the double doors and turned to face Brie.

She was kneeling on the ground, her head bowed, her body open in the pose of submission. He stopped for a moment to appreciate the beauty of her pose before approaching her.

"Do you know what that is?" he asked.

"Yes, I've seen them at the clubs before. I believe it's called a Sabian."

He laughed. "Close, but incorrect. You're naming a race of people. This, however, is known as a Sybian."

Rytsar noted her blush at being wrong and defused her embarrassment by adding, "A mistake easily made, *radost moya*. But we wouldn't want to offend an entire group of people, now would we?"

"No, we would not." She giggled, smiling up at him.

"So you've seen them, but this is your first time up close and personal?"

A shy smiled played across her lips. "You know Sir. He's not into mechanical fucking machines. He's all about the sensual touch."

"But have you been curious?" Rytsar persisted.

She unconsciously bit her bottom lip, her body language answering his question for him.

Rytsar smirked. "Let me introduce you to this bad boy," he stated, pointing to the saddle-like seat bound in black leather that hid a very powerful motor inside. "This one is a stallion among sex toys."

She looked at the Sybian with interest, paying particular attention to the electrical cord and control dial. "I know you're supposed to sit on it, but I'm not sure how it works exactly."

"You have to add an attachment," Rytsar explained.

She grinned, her eyes gleaming with curiosity. "What kind of attachment?"

Rytsar nodded toward the large leather box beside the Sybian and held out a key. "Why don't we open it up so you can find out?" He unlocked the top of the box, lifting the lid slowly, but not allowing her to peek inside.

Rytsar pulled out the first two attachments and set the lid back down.

"How many do you have in there?" she asked, giggling.

He only winked.

Brie glanced at the two items in his hands. "They look like chocolatey goodness…"

Rytsar held up both a smoothed and nubbed attachment. "These two fit on your stallion for those times when you only desire clitoral stimulation or your Master doesn't want you to take your clothes off."

"Oh…" Brie leaned closer. "How do they feel to the touch?"

He held one out to her. "Judge for yourself."

Brie ran her fingers over it lightly. "It's soft, kind of like silicone." She immediately turned her attention on the small rounded bits at the front. "Look at all those little nubs of pleasure." She gazed up at Rytsar. "I bet they do a number on a girl's clit."

He smirked in answer.

Laying the two attachments down, Rytsar picked out another from the box—a thin little rod in the shape of a human finger.

Brie giggled when she examined it closely. "So is this how a girl gets fingered by the stallion?"

Without answering, Rytsar slid a thin plastic rod onto the machine for rigidity before slipping the attachment over it.

He grabbed the dial, turning on the rotator at its slowest speed. The look on Brie's face when she saw it begin to rotate in a circular motion, was priceless. He then switched on the vibration and her eyes widened.

"Ohh…"

He increased both the rotation and the intensity of the vibration. Brie drew closer like a moth to a flame. Turning both dials on high, he watched with satisfaction as her jaw fell open. The impressive sound of the motor ramped up and the Sybian's spirited vibrations filled the room.

"O M G!" Brie said, slapping her cheeks with her hands, her lips making a perfect "O".

Now that she'd been introduced to the power behind the machine, he wanted to familiarize her with the many variations available to her.

Turning off the Sybian, Rytsar pulled out a cock-shaped attachment from the box. "Can you imagine the fun you could have with this, *radost moya?*"

"I can," she said, sounding eager.

He set it down beside the others and took out another with a ball on the end. "What about this?"

"What is it?" she laughed.

"A G-spot stimulator."

"Oh my…" she gasped, having new respect for it.

He laid it down and picked up another. "Now if your Master is feeling particularly wicked, he can attach the larger G-spot stimulator."

Brie squirmed where she knelt, obviously turned on by the idea.

Rytsar set it down and pulled out the next with a naughty grin. "And if you are hungry for more cock, this is a nice large one."

She nodded enthusiastically. "I like!"

He pulled out the next with a wink. "And if large isn't enough, then you can have extra-large."

"Oh, now that could be fun."

He set it down and reached in for another. "And if you are feeling particularly adventurous, there is the jumbo-size." Rytsar pulled it out slowly to tease her.

"Now *that* reminds me of Boa and Master Anderson," she cooed.

He held up the beast of a phallus to her and asked, "You really think you could take it?"

Brie's eyes sparkled with delight when she answered. "I would definitely be up for the challenge. I can't even begin to imagine what that will feel like on full blast."

Rytsar gestured to the extensive line of attachments. "I chose the darker set for you because I knew it would contrast nicely against your skin."

"And you know I love chocolate..." she replied breathlessly as she took them all in.

He reached into the box for the final one.

"What?! There's more?"

"I saved the best for last. You can use this one whenever you are feeling particularly lonesome for me," he said as he revealed the doubled-headed attachment.

"Double penetration? You're the absolute best!" she gushed. Brie looked up at him lustfully, her libido kindled and ready to be set on fire. "How shall we begin?"

He commanded her to stand up and cupped her chin, leaning in close to graze those luscious lips with his own. "You give each one a kiss while you carefully pack them back into the box."

She looked at him, suddenly suspicious. "Why?"

"Because your good doctor has banned it while you are pregnant."

"No, no, no..." she cried out in misery.

Rytsar couldn't help taking pleasure in the depth of her disappointment, so carefully and lovingly crafted by him. Her sad expression as she kissed each toy and placed it in the wooden box warmed his heart and loins.

Although she would not be enjoying the wonders of the Sybian tonight, he was not going to let her suffer for long. Today, she would know blessed release.

"Well done, *radost moya*," he praised as he locked the box and placed the key in her hand. "Consider this a gift for you and your Master...once the babe is born, of course."

"Thank you, Rytsar," she answered forlornly, unable to hide her bitter disappointment.

"Find a safe place for the key and come to bed," he ordered as he began to undress.

Brie slipped the key into her purse and dutifully joined him on the bed, burying herself under the blankets and curling into a ball.

"What's this?" he complained.

"I'm sad," she whimpered from under the covers.

Rytsar grinned as he took his Magic Wand out from the nightstand drawer and plugged it in before switching it on.

Instantly the covers flew off. Brie stared at the toy with a look of longing.

"Are you sad now?"

She gave him a crooked smile. "Only if you tell me the doctor banned the Hitachi as well."

Rytsar burst out laughing, shaking his head slowly. Growling lustfully under his breath, he commanded, "Lie back and I will show you exactly what's allowed."

She laid her head on the pillow and stared up at him. The look in her eyes was full of angst and unfulfilled need.

He fed off it as he separated her thighs and pressed the vibrating head against her swollen clit. Her passionate moan the instant the wand made contact, sent his libido into overdrive.

Rytsar ignored his own sexual needs, concentrating solely on her. Claiming Brie's lips, he continued the pressure on her clit as his finger slowly entered her scorching hot depths. He began caressing her G-spot slowly, thoughtfully.

He gazed into those honey-colored eyes as she stiffened in his arms and came for him.

"Good girl," he murmured. "It has been a long time for you."

She nodded as he pulled the Hitachi away. Brie lifted her head and kissed him on the lips.

"It is not healthy to ignore your sexual needs. That part of your being requires nurturing and care. To deny it is to neglect an essential part of your spirit." He bit down on her throat as he swirled his finger inside her, teasing her G-spot. Soon, Rytsar felt her ravenous body tense before exploding in another orgasm, her inner muscles squeezing his finger with powerful rhythmic pulses. "You have been cruel to yourself, haven't you?"

She moaned again, her entire body trembling as he coaxed another orgasm from her. He felt for the girl, knowing her energy and attention had been focused on Thane since the crash. It was his sincere pleasure to give this gift of release.

It took hours before Brie was completely sated.

Brie lay on his bed, drenched in sweat, her pussy hot pink and swollen, her eyes glazed—her lust fully quenched.

Rytsar lay down beside her, feeling proud of his accomplishment. Not once had he given in to his own lust, and yet he too felt satisfied. There was a certain level of sexual fulfillment to be gained in pleasing another.

He snorted. Hell, was he suddenly channeling Brie's submissive side?

"Thank you, Rytsar," she murmured, her eyelids fluttering as she looked up at him.

He gazed down at her and smiled. "My pleasure, *radost moya*."

She was asleep a few seconds later. Chuckling to himself, Rytsar covered her up and mused as he stroked her long hair.

What he wouldn't have given to share moments like this with Tatianna…

His heart ached at the thought.

Seeing her face again would be worth a thousand deaths. Settling down, he gathered Brie into his arms and joined her in slumber, feeling more at peace with Fate.

Rytsar woke just before dawn.

He looked down at Brie before he left the bed and noted the slight smile gracing her lips as she slept.

Success.

He left her and headed out to greet the ocean. The icy chill of the water shocked his system and invigorated his soul. Today he would be seeing Lilly again, and gifting her with something she would never forget. It would live with her day in and day out for the rest of her life, causing cold sweats whenever it came to mind.

Such a simple and effective form of torture…

He pushed up out of the churning ocean waves and roared with sheer excitement.

It would be a spectacular day.

Rytsar was gratified to note Brie's many glances and shy smiles upon his return. A satisfied woman was a beautiful creature indeed.

"Good morning, Rytsar," Brie said, twisting in place where she stood.

"It is a good morning, isn't it?"

She played with her hair, blushing under his intense stare. "Will we be heading out soon to see Sir?"

"Actually, I have some business to take care of the next few days. Titov and Grigory will be attending to you in my stead."

Rather than question him on it, Brie accepted his answer—although it was easy to see she was unhappy about it.

"You look as if you have something to say."

She glanced away nervously before meeting his gaze. "Please be careful."

He chuckled lightly, touched by her concern. "Have no fear. I am going to be a *dyadya*. I will take no unnecessary chances."

"Good, because I couldn't bear losing you."

Rytsar could tell she was still teetering on the edge emotionally, and assured her. "We are bonded now. You are never getting rid of me."

She stared at him for several moments before nodding.

Brie turned to Titov and asked, "Do you mind if we go now? I'm anxious to see my husband."

"Certainly," Titov answered, calling Grigory to join them.

Brie turned back to Rytsar. "When can I expect to see you again?"

"Tonight, and every night, until my business is concluded."

She beamed him a smile as she walked over to him. Standing on tiptoes, Brie wrapped her hands behind his neck and whispered, "Then stay safe, my Russian knight." She slowly let go of him before turning to follow Titov.

As Rytsar watched Brie leave, he smiled to himself.

This Russian knight is about to kick ass.

Punishment

Rytsar returned to the compound, anxious for the fun to begin. He was pleased to find Lilly in a foul mood.

"How dare you!"

A bald, naked creature with a giant round belly came rushing at him, screeching like a banshee, her arms flailing wildly in a desperate attempt to hit him.

Rytsar laughed, having no difficulty holding her at bay. The hideous fiend standing before him looked much more akin to the ugly soul hidden underneath.

With her claws cut, she had nothing to attack with. He grabbed her wrist and twisted it behind her back, forcing her to kneel on the floor while she begged for him to stop.

Rytsar did not loosen his hold, demanding her silence. When she continued to whine, he tightened his grip until she cried for mercy. "Okay, okay…enough. I'll be quiet."

Rytsar waited until she became completely still, not loosening his grip, and asked her, "Did you enjoy the food?"

Lilly looked up at him and snarled, her expression made that much more grotesque by the heavy lines of makeup smeared on her face.

"You mean that gray viscous crap? It's *not* food."

"But it is. In fact, it was specially formulated by a top obstetrician. The 'shake' might not be tasty or have a pleasant texture, but I assure you that the baby is getting exactly what it needs."

"I fucking hate you!"

"How arrogant of you to think I care."

Rytsar released his hold on her and watched Lilly scramble back to her feet, rubbing her arm, which had come dangerously close to popping out of its socket.

"Are you planning to ask me more stupid questions?" Lilly sneered.

Rytsar looked her up and down with open revulsion. "Again, you amaze me with how obtuse you are."

She backed away from him and growled. "I'm not the stupid one, you idiot!"

"Let me make this perfectly clear for you," he said in a patronizing tone. "I gave you the opportunity to tell the truth before. I would not waste my breath asking again. You lied to me, and now you will pay the consequence. There's no escaping it."

Her eyes widened in fear before she snorted. "Nice try, you wannabe commie. You think that cutting off my hair and clipping my nails is going to break me? Huh! Just goes to show how truly dim-witted you are."

Rytsar raised his eyebrow but said nothing.

She gestured to her naked state. "And you think I

care if I have clothes? I've nothing to hide. I stand before you proud and unashamed," she said, caressing her bulging belly, "because I am carrying Thane's child. I can't wait until he finds out how you treated the mother of his own flesh and blood."

"It is unnecessary to perpetuate the lie, *pizda*," he replied coldly. Rytsar turned from her and started toward the door.

"Oh, that's it. Run away, you fucking coward!" He noticed that she did not try to follow him. Her shoulder would continue hurting for days, even though she was trying hard not to show it.

Rytsar turned and smiled pleasantly once he reached the door. "I have a gift for you. It is something that holds special meaning for me. I hope it burns a hole into your heart."

"What? What are you going to burn?" she cried.

Rytsar ignored her as he closed the door.

"What the hell are you planning?" she screamed, fear tainting her voice.

He slid the lock back into place with a satisfied smile.

"Yegor," he ordered, "begin the serenade. Turn it off at exactly nine at night and begin again at six the next morning. We want the mother to get rest for the innocent's sake."

"How loud would you like it, Rytsar?"

He thought for a moment. "Keep it at a level loud enough to interrupt her thoughts."

"Very well."

"While the music must never stop until the designated hour, you may turn it down whenever you work with her or when I enter the room."

"Does that mean you will be back tomorrow?"

"Naturally. The fun has just begun…"

As Rytsar walked out of the building, he heard the faint melody of "You Are My Sunshine" start up behind him.

He chuckled to himself.

That simple tune was set to play on a continuous loop for fifteen hours each day as per his instructions until "my sunshine" was the only thing she could think about.

That's right, pizda, no one threatens the life of moye solntse.

Rytsar returned the next day, but before he entered the room he told his men, "Get a bucket of ice water and have the restraints ready."

He waited patiently until they returned with the requested items, listening with dark amusement to the song playing on the other side of the door.

When his men returned, he took the bucket from them and walked inside, smiling at Yegor as he closed the door behind him.

Lilly didn't notice he'd entered the room, having taken a sitting position in a corner with her hands over her ears. When the music was lowered, she slowly uncovered her ears and glanced up.

The look in her eyes was that of a crazed person. "I can't take it anymore!"

Rytsar stared at her without sympathy.

Lilly slowly got up to her feet and stammered, "What…the hell…do you want from me?"

"I want you to suffer."

She gaped at him in horror. "Why? I'm innocent!"

When Rytsar failed to acknowledge her lie, Lilly became more animated, falsely believing that would sway him. Pointing to the valley between her breasts, Lilly cried, "I'm the one who has been wronged here. Me! First I was attacked by my own brother and now I'm being tortured for it."

It was a foolish attempt on her part, but Rytsar let her continue because it amused him.

"*He* attacked *me*—and now Thane needs to man up to that responsibility. Since he can't, his wife must."

Rytsar drenched Lilly with the bucket of ice water.

She screeched and then started sputtering as she scrambled away like a crazed animal, attempting to get as far from Rytsar as she could.

"Enough with the lies," he growled.

"You monster!"

"I am the deliverer of justice, nothing more," he replied with indifference.

Rytsar could see the anger begin to rise up inside her. He was not surprised when she attempted to rush him again. With masculine grace, he caught and immobilized her.

"It appears to me that you require restraints, *suka*."

He whistled, and Yegor entered the room with the leather restraints in his hand.

Rytsar dragged Lilly kicking and screaming to the

bed. When she tried to bite him, he grabbed her jaw and squeezed hard.

She whimpered at the power behind his grasp.

"Don't try that again or I will have your teeth removed."

She didn't make another move to bite him when he let go, and did not resist when Rytsar started strapping her to the bed with Yegor's help. When they were done, she lay spread-eagled before him, the dark triangle of her mound barely visible due to her round belly.

"Are you going to fuck me now?" she demanded and sneered. "Is that it, big boy?"

Rytsar looked at her with open disdain. "I would never lower myself."

She looked at the restraints on her wrists. "Then why would you tie me up, pervert?"

"So you can enjoy the music more fully," he replied with an evil glint in his eye.

"Oh God no. Not that again!" she cried piteously. "Please, no more."

Rytsar and Yegor turned in unison and headed out.

"You bastard. You sick motherfucker!" she screamed after him.

Rytsar smiled at her as if he was bestowing a cherished gift when he shut the door.

Once they exited, he told Yegor, "I want you to turn up the volume a few more decibels."

Yegor smiled. "As you wish."

Rytsar walked down the hallway with a light heart. Torturing Lilly was proving far too entertaining.

When he returned to the compound the next day, Yegor immediately informed him that they'd had to force-feed her every meal.

"Good. We're finally making progress," Rytsar replied.

He entered the room and found Lilly staring up at the ceiling as if dead. While it was a pleasant thought for him, he purposely ruined the illusion by clearing his throat.

She turned her head toward him listlessly.

"I was informed you refused to eat."

"I can't bear it," Lilly whined. "It's disgusting and the texture makes me want to retch."

"Then retch," he answered.

"What about the baby?" she asked, rubbing her stomach.

"My men will gather it up and feed it back to you like a baby bird."

"You're a sick bastard."

"It must be consumed because you are pregnant. I couldn't care less how it gets there," he responded without sympathy.

She curled her nose in a snarl. "Well, I won't eat it!"

"Then it will be forced down your gullet while they pinch your nose closed until you swallow every last spoonful."

"You fucking dickhead!"

Rytsar frowned at her, stating firmly, "You will speak

to me in a respectful manner at all times from now on."

"Like hell I will."

Rytsar left the room and returned a short time later with the bucket.

She shook her head, crying out desperately. "I take it back, I take it bac—"

He slowly dumped the entire bucket of icy water over her head, specifically so she could experience the sensation of drowning.

After she was done coughing and sputtering, Lilly shrieked, "I took it back, you asshole."

Rytsar whistled and handed Yegor the bucket when he entered the room. While he waited, he took pleasure in her desperate pleas.

"I won't do it again, I promise. Please, don't!"

Upon Yegor's return, Lilly became silent, watching Rytsar like a scared mouse.

He took the bucket from Yegor and turned to face Lilly. "Every incident of disrespect will be followed by swift punishment. Do you understand?"

She looked at the bucket in terror. "Please don't, I'm sorry. I'm sorry!" When he lifted the bucket she screamed, "I'm telling you I'm fucking sorry!"

"You can't get out of being punished by saying you're sorry afterward. It doesn't work that way with me. You were disrespectful twice, therefore you *must* suffer the consequences…twice." Without ceremony, he poured the freezing water over her head.

She whimpered afterward but didn't speak.

"Until tomorrow."

As he was leaving, Lilly called out to him, "I'll tell

you anything you want to know."

He said nothing as he closed the door but smirked when the music started up again and she began howling.

Rytsar told his men, "Let her suffer for another fifteen minutes before you dry her and change the bedding." He smiled broadly. "I think you should see an improvement in her appetite."

He was curious how he would find her the following day. So far he had only employed simple tactics to break her.

There was a deep sense of satisfaction knowing the woman who had drugged Brie and the babe was under his control. All the pain and uncertainty she had inflicted on his friends was now being directed back at her full force, as it should be—without violence.

At first glance, Lilly seemed more compliant when he walked into the room. He felt the change in her demeanor but didn't trust it.

Lilly addressed him as he approached. "Do I need to call you Master or something?"

"You're not worthy."

"Good, because I'm not your damn slave," she muttered, turning away.

"Correct, you are not. You are nothing—insignificant."

The expression on her face showed her offense, but Lilly kept her mouth shut.

"I think we are done here for today," he announced.

As he turned away, Lilly cried out piteously, "Please, don't go."

He didn't miss a step as he walked out the door and slipped the lock into place.

Where she was hoping to incite his sympathy, he only saw red. The image of Brie slumped in a strange man's arms as she was carried off to become a victim at the hands of Lilly was Rytsar's only reality.

Nothing the creature did or said would change that, but he trusted that soon she would open up in the hopes he would show mercy and all his questions could be answered.

When he went to Thane, he was determined to give a full and accurate accounting.

It was a shock for Rytsar when he came the next day and found her completely despondent. She stared upward, a blank expression on her face.

He walked out of the room to question his men.

"Has she been eating?"

"No. She was force-fed each meal."

"Water too?"

"*Da.*"

"Any words or actions from her since I left?"

His men all shook their heads.

"This is a ruse, but I want to play it out. Feed her on schedule and let's see how long she can keep this up."

Rytsar arrived early the next morning, curious what his men would report. Her mental state hadn't changed. She remained almost catatonic, not moving or responding.

He didn't even bother entering her room.

"Let me see the video surveillance."

His men walked him to a room down the hall and together they watched her movements from the day before. Rytsar had to give the creature credit. She remained still for hours each time his men fed her, but there came a point when she couldn't maintain the façade and she began thrashing in the bed.

Rytsar smiled as he pointed at the screen. "That is a maggot about to break."

He knew she would be disappointed when he did not come to visit her and it pleased him. He knew the worry it would cause her, the second doubts, and the extra pain she would suffer keeping still for so long.

The fact that any added suffering she was experiencing was her own doing only made it that much sweeter.

Rytsar took the extra time afforded him that day and spent it shopping—for the babe.

Moye solntse would have everything her little heart desired. It was his duty as her *dyadya*.

Rytsar returned the next day prepared to call her bluff.

Today the creature would taste a little of her own medicine.

"Get the syringe ready," he told Yegor.

While it was being prepared, he instructed his men, "Go in there, make attempts to revive her as you feed her."

Rytsar had them keep the door open so he could observe her while they worked. She remained limp and unresponsive, not struggling even when they poured the concoction down her throat, but he noted she voluntarily swallowed.

Yegor returned with the relaxant. Rytsar had done his research, specifically choosing a medication routinely used with pregnant women. There was no chance of harming the fetus, although Lilly would be unaware of that.

He explained what he wanted Yegor to do and walked in behind him, but stayed a step back to observe.

The men had just finished feeding her and were about to leave when Yegor stopped them. "I require your assistance."

"What's up?"

"The boss just called and told me to dispose of the body."

Rytsar watched closely and noticed Lilly's lips twitching slightly.

"Unbind her wrist," Yegor ordered.

Rytsar noticed she stopped breathing for a moment as they untied her wrist and it fell stiffly to her side.

Yegor grabbed her arm and positioned it to receive the injection. "Too easy a death for this one," he grumbled as he held her arm firmly and slowly eased the needle into her vein.

Lilly cried out the instant he started pushing on the plunger. She thrashed her arm, trying to pull away from Yegor's tight grip, without success.

She screamed at the top of her lungs, "They're trying to kill me! Help, they are trying to kill m—!"

Her cries stopped short when she saw Rytsar standing there. Tears ran down her face as she sniveled. "I don't want to die…"

"You will soon feel the rush of the chemical as it races to your heart."

"No," she cried. "Make it stop! Oh my God, make it stop…"

"Any last words?"

"I'll tell you everything—everything. Please don't kill me."

Rytsar snapped his fingers and Yegor gave him another syringe of saline. Rytsar pushed it in her vein himself and released the harmless liquid into her bloodstream.

She stared at it with wide eyes and looked up at him. "You're saving me?"

"Tell me what I want to know, then I'll decide."

Lilly nodded and actually smiled, the relaxant having a tipsy effect on her. "Well, it all began when I met dreamy Thane in person. That sexy hunk of man meat…" She giggled. "I share my mother's love of Italian hotties and I knew—*knew*—we were meant to be together."

Whispers

Brie had not questioned Rytsar about his daily outings until the day he insisted on going with her to the hospital in the morning. She was quiet the entire drive, but when they were in the room alone with Thane she finally burst.

"Rytsar, you've been so mysterious about Lilly. I believe you've found her, but…"

"But what, *radost moya?*" he asked in a somber tone.

Brie looked nervously at Thane and asked, "You haven't killed her, have you?"

He gave her a grave look. "The innocent inside the creature still lives."

Brie frowned, unsure of the meaning of his answer. "But Lilly is still alive too, right?"

"If you knew what I knew, you would want her dead."

It was as if Thane heard Rytsar's words, because he suddenly started coughing violently as his heart rate shot up to dangerous levels.

Brie ran to Thane's bedside, screaming, "No! Fight

this, Sir. Don't leave me!"

The nurses rushed in, followed by the doctor soon after. Dr. Hessen barked to Rytsar, "Get her out of here."

Rytsar tried to pull Brie away from Thane, but she held on so tightly that by dragging her, he was dragging Thane as well. Understanding Brie was impeding the staff, Rytsar gripped the back of her neck and squeezed.

He felt her tense as she instantly froze in place. Now that he had her attention he stated calmly, "We need to leave now, *radost moya*."

She instantly let go of Sir's hand, and Rytsar whisked her out of the chaos of the room, but Brie didn't go quietly. Screaming, her desperation heartbreaking and real, she cried, "You can't let him die! Don't let him die…"

She clung onto Rytsar once they were in the hallway, burying her head in his chest. Brie began weeping then. "I can't watch. It's too much like Tono."

Rytsar held her tightly, trying to comfort himself as much as Brie. "He will not die. He cannot die," he insisted out loud. But like Brie, he was already imagining the worst.

He began to stroke her hair, attempting to be her comfort when all he wanted to do was yell at the top of his lungs. But as he watched the scene play out through the glass wall, he realized that what they had witnessed was not his demise but a miracle.

"*Radost moya…*"

When she didn't respond, he commanded her to look. Brie took a peek and let out a loud gasp.

The staff were smiling at each other, the ambiance in the room one of joy and not sorrow. As the staff moved about, Rytsar saw the doctor handing the respirator tube to a nurse.

Thane was breathing on his own.

Dr. Hessen came out to speak with them. "He is breathing on his own again, Mrs. Davis. A significant step in his recovery."

"Can I see him?" Brie begged.

"Of course, I—"

Without waiting, Brie rushed back into the room, wiping away her tears as she approached with Rytsar right behind her.

She took Thane's hand and began kissing it over and over again.

He was staring at the ceiling, just as he always had. As far as Rytsar could tell, nothing seemed to have changed other than the breathing tube was gone, leaving Thane breathing on his own.

Rytsar felt a jolt when Thane suddenly turned his head toward Brie and looked directly into her eyes.

Brie just stared at him, completely transfixed, as stunned as Rytsar.

Thane said nothing, and Rytsar began to fear that he didn't recognize her.

As the seconds ticked past, he could see in Brie's expression that she had the same concern.

"Sir?"

Thane blinked a couple of times, and the beat on the monitor increased.

Brie glanced over at Rytsar, her fears easy to read on

her face. Rytsar couldn't reassure her—not now. It was as if his worst fears were coming true. The body might have awakened, but that didn't mean Thane was inside there.

She looked back at her husband, moving closer as she gazed beseechingly into his eyes.

Thane's heart rate suddenly shot up as he met her gaze. In the barest of whispers, hoarse from disuse, he finally spoke.

"Babygirl…"

Brie completely lost it. "Oh Sir, I've missed you so much. So very much!"

Thane said nothing more as they stared into each other's eyes.

Rytsar attempted to leave the room, but Thane caught the movement and looked up at him.

The instant their eyes met, Rytsar felt a flood of relief. He knew without a doubt that Thane recognized him.

"*Moy droog.*"

Before Thane could open his mouth to speak, Rytsar put his hand up. "There is no need to say anything. You are back among the living." He hit his fist against his chest. "Your brother is deeply grateful."

Thane nodded slightly.

Rytsar did not wipe away the tears that escaped and rolled down his face. This was a miraculous moment, and he was not ashamed to cry.

Thane's gaze rested on him for several moments. Rytsar was certain he saw concern in those eyes. There would be time to talk later. Right now, Thane needed time alone with his woman.

Rytsar gave him a curt bow. "I am stepping out for a moment, but do not slip back into a coma, *moy droog*. If you do, I will beat the shit out of you."

Thane gave him the barest of smiles. It was obvious that everything was an effort for him. It would be a tough fight ahead.

Rytsar grinned down at Brie and announced with bravado, "Did I not tell you he would be fine?"

Brie melted his heart, that inner joy he knew and loved bursting out in her smile.

"He's back!"

While Rytsar gave the lovebirds time alone, he made a point to hunt down Nurse Abby to get a better idea of what lay ahead in Thane's recovery.

Rytsar didn't return for several hours, wanting to give his friends time to get reacquainted after such a long separation.

He used that extended time to speak to Titov about beginning preparations for Thane to return home. Rytsar shook his head after he got off the phone, still not quite believing his brother had really come out of the coma. There was a part of him that feared this moment of hope would be stolen away from them in the blink of an eye.

When he walked back into Thane's room hours later and was confronted with an empty bed, his very first thought was that Thane had passed.

Fortunately, a nurse walked in with new bedsheets and saw the devastation on his face. "Oh no, don't worry, Mr. Durov. Your brother was moved to another floor. We have a patient in need of this one."

Rytsar regained his composure—barely. "In the name of all that is Holy, what is the room number?"

She smiled compassionately. "Come with me, and I will look that up for you."

Rytsar followed her out and nodded to the other nurses as he waited. Abby came up and put her hand on his shoulder. "Although I will miss your face, I am happy for the reason."

"As am I, Nurse Abby."

She blushed when he flashed her a rare, totally heartfelt smile.

"Would you like me to show you to his room?"

"Could you?"

"Of course, it would be my pleasure." Nurse Abby looked to the other nurses and asked, "Do you mind covering for me?"

The others readily agreed, showering Rytsar with well-wishes and good-byes as he headed out the ICU doors. As they were walking down the hall, Rytsar asked her, "Is alcohol permitted as a gift to the hospital staff?"

She glanced up at him and laughed. "Well, I'm sure no one would turn it down."

"Good. You have taken exemplary care of my brother."

"There's no need to thank us with gifts, Mr. Durov," she assured him. "It's our job and passion."

"Ah, but those who do their jobs well should be

compensated, don't you agree?"

Abby's laughter echoed down the hallway. "You know, Mr. Durov, when you first came to our hospital, I didn't like you."

"Really? Because I'm Russian?"

"No, it's not that at all. The fact you hit Mr. Nosaka, a complete gentleman, didn't sit right with me. We all assumed you were a total jerk."

"What changed your poor opinion of me?" he asked with an amused smirk.

"I'll admit it took a while, but I noticed your attentiveness with Mrs. Davis, and on several occasions Mr. Davis reacted when you entered the room. It made it easier to give you a chance."

"Although you thought ill of me, you still qualify for a gift."

Abby giggled as the elevator doors opened on the new floor and she guided him through the maze of hallways.

"May I ask something personal, Mr. Durov?"

"Perhaps."

She paused for a moment before continuing. "Are you the man who rescued that girl in Russia? Because you seem awfully familiar to me."

"Perhaps."

Abby grinned. "I think I have my answer. To be honest, I feel honored to meet you in person."

Rytsar waved away her admiration. "I only did what was right."

"Not many people choose to step in to help someone. We see it all the time here. It takes a rare individual to risk themselves for someone else."

"To do nothing is a coward's response."

Abby shrugged. "Still, not many people do. So let me say thank you on behalf of young girls everywhere. May what you did inspire others to open their eyes and take a stand when they see human trafficking."

"May many find the courage to stand up for the innocent," he agreed somberly.

Abby suddenly stopped in the middle of the hallway and gestured to room 250. "Here's Mr. Davis's new room."

Rytsar paused for a moment before entering. Putting a finger under her chin, he tilted her head up to look deep into her eyes. "If you do not hear it enough, you are the real hero. Working every day to protect the lives under your care, without recognition—day after day, year after year. *That* is the real mark of a hero."

Abby stared into his eyes with gratitude and the unmistakable look of desire. "I won't forget you, Mr. Durov."

He answered with mock arrogance, "I *am* hard to forget."

She laughed lightly as she turned and started back up to the ICU. He didn't miss the extra sway in her hips as she walked away.

Confessions

Rytsar entered the hospital room and was relieved to see Brie sitting beside Sir's bed, still smiling.

"I take it the peasant is doing well enough to change locations on me."

Brie's eyes sparkled. "He is, Rytsar! Although Sir can't really speak and his muscles are weak, he is doing well."

Rytsar shot Thane a quick glance. "Would you agree, comrade?"

Thane nodded, but Rytsar could read the distress in his eyes.

"*Moy droog*, there are things I must tell you."

Thane nodded again, clearly interested in hearing what he had to say.

"*Radost moya*, would you mind giving me a few moments alone with my brother?"

As much as Brie wanted to honor his wish, he could tell she was reluctant to leave Thane's side. It was quite possible that she also feared that this was only temporary and that she might come back to find him unresponsive again.

"I will get you as soon as I am done berating my brother for scaring the crap out of me." Rytsar winked at her to assure Brie everything would be okay.

Brie pursed her lips, forcing herself to accept her exile, and leaned over to kiss Thane. "I miss you already."

Thane lifted his arm weakly, his hand trembling from the effort as he went to touch her cheek. Brie grabbed it and pressed it against her. With a will of iron, she forced herself to break away and leave the room.

Rytsar took the chair she had been using and turned it around before sitting down. "We have much to talk about but first…before anything else, you must know I would have been here the instant I heard about your crash. But that's the catch. I was not informed of the accident until a few weeks ago. Whether it was a legitimate mistake or by design, I am still not convinced, but know that my absence was not of my own doing, *moy droog*."

Thane shook his head, his eyes communicating that he was troubled by Rytsar's words.

"Hah!" he said dismissively, not wanting to add to Thane's distress. "In the end, it is not important because I am here now, *radost moya* is safe, and you are wide awake."

Thane's eyes drifted to the door.

"Yes, it is serious, *moy droog*. Your creature of a half-sister planned to do Brie and the babe great harm, and hurt you in the process." Rytsar shook his head, finding it hard to voice the truth aloud but knowing his friend needed to know.

"Before I say any more, know that she is being held in a secure facility. I have kept my word to your woman not to harm the child she carries, but that does not mean I have held back my wrath. This woman deserves to die, and we both know she will continue to be a threat to you both until she draws her last breath."

He leaned in close and growled. "A snake whose life has been spared has no concept of gratitude. Its only instinct is to strike its prey dead."

Thane closed his eyes, a pained expression playing across his face.

"I have placed a fear so deep inside her that she will think twice about harming my family, but I cannot guarantee it will last. Her hatred for Brie and her obsession with you are of equal and dangerous degrees."

Thane opened his eyes, staring intently at Rytsar.

"With forceful persuasion, I have gotten her to confess several important things. Are you interested in hearing them now or would you rather wait until you have had a few days to recover?"

Thane's harsh stare answered his question.

"Very well, but I warn you. Such knowledge may prove a hindrance to your recovery, for to know such things and not be able to take action is detrimental to the soul."

With difficulty, Thane croaked out the words, "Tell me."

"All right, *moy droog*. But you have been warned." He leaned even closer, speaking to Thane in low tones, not wanting to be overheard if anyone should happen to walk in.

"From what I've learned, your half-sister became obsessed with you when you met the first time in person. Her interest in you was not just because of the money, although that was a deciding factor. This creature… She's truly depraved, comrade. When she found you extremely attractive, she completely dismissed the fact you both share a mother."

Thane gave Rytsar a look of disgust.

"I know, but it gets worse. When she left to go back to New York, she started fantasizing about you. Her infatuation became a sick obsession when she happened across a new employee at her office, who resembled you. She doggedly pursued the man and convinced him to cheat on his wife—but that wasn't enough for her. She eventually coaxed him into renting a studio apartment for their clandestine encounters.

"Determined to make this man into the image of you, she insisted he take on the Dominant role, but what she had failed to realize is that some men are violent at heart and, given the opportunity to unleash it freely, such power inspires only cruelty and abuse.

"The harsh intercourse finally became too much for her but instead of breaking it off, she sought vengeance by going to his wife and confronting her in person about the affair. Needless to say, her actions resulted in an equally devastating reaction. Thinking herself so clever, she convinced the man to meet her at the studio apartment with plans to blackmail him for money by threatening his job.

"But she misjudged what would happen that night when he finally showed up. Before she could defend herself, he attacked, releasing his rage by violently fucking her. He left her on the floor crying, warning her that if she ever contacted him or his family again, he would end her.

"Taking his threat seriously, she chose not to contact him when she discovered she was pregnant with his child. Instead of going to the police, she crafted a plan to ensnare you—her true obsession.

"When the creature joined you in China, she'd already set into place the elements by which she would blackmail you, but her inexperience with the herbs she drugged you with almost cost your life. Her liberal use of them in your drinks that night caused you to overdose, and she immediately abandoned the plan...until Brie showed up.

"Seeing your woman pushed her into a jealous rage. She became crazed with the idea of making you hers and made her accusation against you in front of Brie, convinced it would be enough to tear the two of you apart.

"In her perverted mind, she believed that by claiming the child was yours, it made it so. She expected Brie to renounce you and leave the picture. Being that you are a gentleman, she'd convinced herself that you would insist on taking care of her out of guilt and raise the child as your own. But with time, you would fall madly in love."

Thane's eyes narrowed.

"I agree, the creature is warped in the head, and I could have a level of sympathy for her, but for what came after."

Rytsar got up and started pacing, trying to discharge the seething rage building inside him.

"Livid when Brie stuck beside you and you cut off all contact from her, she became convinced Brie was the reason you were not responding favorably to her plight. That's when she decided to blackmail you and sent the letter to force your hand."

Rytsar growled, thinking back to that moment when Lilly had spilled out the darkest part of her soul to him…

"You won't like my answer." Lilly looked up at him, a drunken smile on her lips caused by the relaxant flowing in her veins.

"That is irrelevant," he told her.

"Would…would you untie me first?"

"Only the arms." His tone was curt and emotionless as he undid the other binding. It allowed the spineless creature to sit up, but kept her restrained and under his control.

"So you want to know why I came to LA?" Lilly grinned and then huffed in frustration. "I thought it would be easier to manipulate with my brother dying in the hospital."

Rytsar corrected, "You are only allowed to address him as Mr. Davis. You are unworthy to call him brother."

She looked up at Rytsar with a hint of defiance.

He had only to look at her arm with a raised eyebrow for her to squelch it. Looking down at her lap, she continued. What came out of her mouth raised the hairs on his neck.

"When it proved more stupid than I anticipated, I was forced to take action."

"Go on," he told her, now realizing that when she referred to "it" she was speaking of Brie.

"So the minute I realized it had no plans to hand over the money, I called in an old associate to help remove the problem."

"The problem being Mrs. Davis?" he stated, narrowing his eyes.

Lilly looked up at Rytsar and answered cryptically, "In a manner of speaking…" giggling as she said it.

"Clarify," he demanded, fighting the urge to backhand her.

Lilly held on to her belly in a gesture of protection. "Promise you won't hurt me if I tell you."

Rytsar had no patience for her weak dramatics and warned her, "Speak or we end this now."

She blurted, "I separated it from the others so Reese could slip the drugs into her drink." She then muttered to herself, "Should have known that fucker would screw it up…"

"*What* were you planning to do to Mrs. Davis?"

She stared up at him blankly, her words devoid of all emotion. "I was going to eliminate the fetus."

Kill moye solntse? The she-devil has to die!

It took everything in Rytsar not to go into berserker mode right then and there. He would have snapped the *suka*'s neck if there hadn't been a child.

Although he was raging under the stoic exterior he presented, he held himself in check. It was imperative to learn everything before he unleashed his wrath.

"I warned you that you wouldn't like it," she said, eyeing him warily. "I knew you'd be upset, seeing how careful you are with my own precious baby." She looked down at her belly and cooed, rubbing her stomach—forcing him to acknowledge that violence against her would result in the innocent's death.

Pushing forward with the interrogation, he demanded, "What were your plans for Mrs. Davis?"

Lilly let out a smug little laugh that set his nerves on edge. "I was going to make all its dreams come true."

"How?"

"Reese was going to fly it to a new owner in the Middle-East so it could bask in the life of a true slave."

"You were going to *sell* her?" he asked, every muscle in his body tensing.

"I see it more as a simple change of ownership," she said with a laugh. "This would give it the opportunity to whore itself to its heart's content, while Than—Mr. Davis," she quickly amended, "put his energy where it belongs—on his son."

"*That* is not his child," Rytsar stated harshly, looking at her bulging stomach.

"But with time it would have been," she insisted. "You see, the genetic test I have proves it, and with the baby's daddy looking so similar to him, as well as what happened in China... Well, with time he would come to believe it and claim the child as his own."

"Mr. Davis is not stupid, *pizda*. He would have insisted on a test by a qualified doctor and your lie would have been exposed for the insanity it is."

"But I would have happily gone to any doctor or hospital he wanted. All I'd have to do is switch the results. Nothing is impossible if you have the right connections," she added with a wicked smile.

Although Rytsar agreed with her last statement, her perverse fantasy was repulsive. "Mr. Davis is your half-brother. This dream you have of being his pseudo-wife is not only demented but revolting in every way."

Lilly looked wounded and answered defensively, "Being half-siblings means nothing when you're talking about the affairs of the heart."

"Of which you have none. Have you forgotten the child you planned to murder and the woman you were going to enslave? The only justice I see is you suffering the very things you planned for her."

Lilly grabbed at her stomach. "But you promised you wouldn't hurt me!"

Rytsar grabbed Lilly's arms roughly to tie her back up. He forced himself not to wrap his hands around her throat in the process. The need to strangle her was so strong that he had to back away once he was finished.

"Mercy! I cry mercy for my child," she begged.

"Granted. Instead of eliminating you right now, you shall remain here until you give birth. Any woman who could plan the death of someone else's child cannot be trusted with her own. Consider yourself lucky for the extra time granted."

He left Lilly alive—reluctantly.

Her crazed screams brought him no pleasure as he slammed the door and told his men to turn the music up to full blast.

Rytsar looked at Thane, feeling deeply troubled that he would have to share this news with him.

"I find it difficult to tell you more. I am not able to eliminate the threat for the time being and you will only be able to lie here with the knowledge of what she tried to do." He looked at his own palms and lamented, "Both of our hands are tied for different reasons."

Thane stared at him and whispered hoarsely, "Brother."

Rytsar nodded. It was Thane's right to know.

Wrapping his hand around Thane's in an act of solidarity, Rytsar laid out what Lilly had confessed to him.

There were moments during the conversation that Thane closed his eyes, unable to accept what he heard. Rytsar waited until he indicated he was ready to continue. The reality that they had almost lost Brie and the baby was hard to stomach. The dominant, protective side of their personalities couldn't handle that truth.

"Why didn't you tell me sooner, *moy droog?*" Rytsar accused. "I could have squashed the creature before she had the chance to harm Brie."

Thane shook his head, but Rytsar clearly read the remorse in his eyes.

Suddenly feeling guilty, Rytsar realized he was equally at fault and admitted, "I am not being fair to you…"

Thane's eyes narrowed.

He chuckled sadly. "The truth, *moy droog,* is that I am also guilty of keeping things from you in an attempt to protect *radost moya*. Like true brothers, we share the same flaw."

Thane frowned and squeezed his hand weakly, demanding an explanation.

Rytsar looked him in the eye. "The situation involving the maggot I killed has become complicated. The Kozlov brothers are seeking revenge because it turned out he was their second cousin once removed. Although they'd never met in person, it's made a convenient excuse for vengeance against me."

Thane nodded slowly in understanding, knowing his connection with the Kozlov family.

"I thought I was safe," Rytsar confessed. "But now I see the tides turning and I cannot stop what is coming." He slapped his other hand against Thane's and held tight. "But I promise with every breath still left in me that I will not let *radost moya* suffer for what happened in Russia."

Thane furrowed his brow.

"No. My people never broke their silence, but the girl's confession gained the interest of the *bratva*. When the maggot was identified as missing, the Kozlov brothers eventually put two and two together. You know our history, brother, and with their patriarch dead, there's nothing to stop them now."

Thane's expression set Rytsar on edge.

"I'm sorry, *moy droog*. Too much information to process when you've only just rejoined the living."

His comrade shook his head and croaked out the word with difficulty, "Truth."

Rytsar accepted his assurance. "For better or worse, I

won't keep information from you anymore. The Kozlov brothers desire my death as payment for the maggot. My only option is to avoid capture and attempt to convince them otherwise."

The look of sorrow that Thane gave him echoed his own emotions when he thought he'd lost Thane.

"I vow not to go down without a fight but, if the worst should happen, do not mourn for me. I will be with Tatianna, and will sup at my mother's table again."

Thane shook his head, forcing out the word, "Coward…"

Rytsar smirked. "Fine, you peasant bastard. I will fight as hard as you have. We are brothers after all. Stubborn to the depths of our dark souls."

A faint smile briefly played on Thane's lips.

"Should I give you a few moments to process before I go get your woman?"

Thane nodded and closed his eyes.

Rytsar left Thane feeling uneasy. Having just awakened after months in a coma, his brother needed to focus on himself. Instead, Thane had been forced to carry not only the burden of Lilly's treachery, but Rytsar's own uncertain future.

He found Brie waiting just outside the door. He stopped her from going in, whispering, "He needs some time to himself."

Rytsar had to push her to the waiting room, where he sat her down.

"What's wrong?" she asked.

"He needs a few moments to process."

"Does he seem fully aware to you?"

"*Da.*"

"I think so too. It's been so long since I've looked into his eyes and seen him looking back…" Tears pooled as she said it.

Rytsar wrapped her up in his arms, grateful that this day had finally come for both of them. "I know it has been hard, and there is still much work ahead, but you and I have every reason to rejoice."

Brie pressed her cheek against his shoulder, tears falling as she confessed, "I have waited for this day from the very first moment I saw him in the hospital. I've fought so hard and for so long that I'm scared to believe it's real."

Tatianna

R ytsar lay in bed that night with Brie asleep in his arms, feeling more relaxed than he had in years. He'd lulled her to sleep sharing his story about the day Tatianna answered the door at the tender age of sixteen—the day he'd finally noticed her for the woman she would become.

What Rytsar hadn't told Brie was that had been the moment he'd became utterly obsessed with the girl.

He'd played hard to get at first, choosing not to visit as often and appearing nonchalant whenever their paths happened to cross. Inside, however, his Dominant was raging to possess her and Tatianna didn't make it easy for him, flirting with the other boys when she didn't feel she was getting enough of his attention.

Oh, that girl… Her arched eyebrows expressing everything her lips did not say.

Tatianna wanted him—needed him—but that Russian sparrow was too proud to admit it. Instead, she'd glance at him as she playfully teased Titov's many friends, hoping to catch Rytsar's eye.

What she didn't understand was that he was a Durov. Her fate had been sealed that day, just as it had for his mother all those years ago.

No amount of posturing on Tatianna's part would change the fact Rytsar had chosen her for his mate. He knew, despite all her pretense, that she longed to be possessed by him. It was the reason he waited patiently, looking forward to her eighteenth birthday, when he would stake his official claim and she would be his—and his alone.

That insatiable need to possess her stirred his soul.

He understood now what his father must have gone through when he'd met Rytsar's mother for the first time. She'd never had a chance, but what Rytsar had failed to realize until now was neither had his father.

At nineteen, Rytsar was remarkably stubborn. Even though Tatianna was of legal age in Russia, he had bided his time, wanting to give her the chance to mature into the fine woman she was destined to become. He didn't want her to submit to him as a Dominant until she was ready and willingly to give herself to it freely.

Rytsar had decided to surprise Tatianna on her eighteenth birthday. He would come to her parents' home dressed in a tailored suit and make his formal declaration of intent. Rytsar planned to sway her father with his sincerity and charm her mother with his smile.

Although the family knew him only as Titov's childhood friend, he would make certain they understood he had separated himself from their son in recent months because of his association with the unsavory youth that made up Russia's disenfranchised male population.

Rytsar knew that Titov aligning himself with the fringes of organized crime, would eventually lead to his destruction—it was only a matter of time—and he'd tried to warn Titov on several occasions but his friend refused to listen.

Whereas Tatianna's family was part of the working class, Rytsar came from a long family linage of well-respected aristocrats who did not entangle themselves in the underbelly of Moscow.

Her parents respected Rytsar's family history, but he would make sure they understood he was also a man of ambition. He planned to make a name for himself beyond his family surname—on his own terms that had nothing to do with his father.

While Titov was off sowing his wild oats, Rytsar was concentrating on his future. He knew exactly where he was headed and who he wanted by his side. He'd already purchased the suit, a smoky gray ensemble accented with a dark red tie.

He'd also picked out the ring he would slip onto her finger…

Everything was set, the die had been cast, and all he had to do was wait and be patient.

Rytsar was surprised, however, when an unexpected opportunity presented itself. He'd knocked on the door with the excuse of wanting to see Titov, knowing he would not be home.

When Tatianna opened the door, her eyes widened in pleasure and she blushed. "It's you!"

Rytsar shrugged, trying to act interested but aloof.

Her smile grew. "I'm so glad to see you."

This was the first time she'd been so forward with him and he wondered at the cause. "Any particular reason?" he asked with a smirk.

"The house is empty." She giggled self-consciously. "I'm all alone."

Suddenly his interest was piqued. "When will your family be back?"

"Not for hours," she said, moving aside to invite him in.

Rytsar stepped across the threshold without hesitation. Although he had no intention of taking her innocence just yet, there was no reason not to introduce her to the pleasures that awaited their future coupling.

"A lot can happen in a couple of hours, little girl."

"I'm not little," Tatianna protested. As if to prove it, she asked, "Would you like something to drink?"

"Vodka."

She grinned. "Of course. What else would a good Russian have?"

"A taste of Tatianna," he answered with a wicked grin.

Tatianna blushed deeply as she disappeared into the kitchen. Rytsar made himself at home in the parlor. It was the first time the place had been quiet in all the years he'd been here. It tended to be filled with her family and extended relatives, so this was an extremely unusual turn of events.

She came back out with a bottle of vodka and a single glass.

He tsked disapprovingly. "Get yourself a glass, Tatianna. I never drink alone."

She raised a beautifully arched eyebrow in amusement, but turned around and went back to get the second glass. Upon her return, Rytsar took the bottle and filled both glasses, handing her one.

After a traditional toast, he poured another glass so he could add his own. "To time spent together—alone."

"To the rare treat," she agreed, raising her glass to him.

He winked at his beauty as he downed the vodka and set the empty tumbler on the table.

Tatianna blushed again and looked away, clearly smitten.

Rytsar knew he would have to watch himself with her. He was far too aroused to let his guard down. Since he'd started playing with submissives at the age of fifteen, under his father's critical eye, he already knew much about the female form, including how to provoke and incite it.

But this was Tatianna—an innocent. He wanted to experience something completely different with her. He could not allow his past experiences to taint this first encounter.

Knowing he had little time to waste, Rytsar stated boldly, "I would like to taste your lips."

"Anton!" Tatianna protested, her cheeks turning a deep shade of red. No one called him Anton anymore except his mother, but he found it oddly thrilling coming from her lips.

Rytsar held his hands up in mock surprise. "What?"

"You don't address a lady like that."

"I beg to differ, *vorobyshek*."

She rolled her eyes flirtatiously. "Now you're calling me by a pet name?"

Rytsar moved closer to her. "Naturally, little sparrow."

She would have protested further, but he grasped her chin and planted a kiss on those pouty pink lips. The chemistry between them was dangerous, and he had to pull away. "Do you feel it, Tatianna?"

"What?" she whispered.

"The electricity between us."

She only nodded as she stared at his lips, obviously entranced by the kiss.

"Would you like me to kiss you again?"

"*Pozhaluista.*"

Hearing her murmur "please" was charming, and this time Rytsar rested his hand on her throat as he kissed her, his cock responding to her taste and proximity.

"Oh, Anton…" she murmured, reluctant to break the embrace when he pulled away to sit back on the couch.

It would be so easy to take her right now. She was willing, his manhood certainly wanted the connection, and they had the whole place to themselves…

Deciding there was no harm in taking a peek, he went to undo the buttons on her blouse, longing to touch her bare skin.

Tatianna stilled as he began slowly undoing each button, holding her breath as he progressed lower and lower. "Breathe, my little sparrow."

When the last button was undone, Rytsar pushed back the thin material of her blouse to expose her delicate shoulders. He leaned in and kissed one, lightly biting it afterward.

Goosebumps rose on her skin from the contact.

Rytsar stared into her eyes as he slipped off the bra strap. Each movement one step closer to freeing her breasts from their feminine constraints.

Tatianna started breathing again in shallow little pants. It helped remind him how inexperienced she was.

Moving more slowly, Rytsar reached around and undid her bra, letting it fall gently to her lap. She bit her bottom lip, afraid to look up at him. His eyes drifted to her naked chest—his mate finally exposed.

Rytsar reached out and touched the swell of her breast, lightly rubbing her erect nipple with his thumb.

Tatianna closed her eyes, concentrating on his touch as her breath became even more shallow and rapid.

"You are fully woman," he growled lustfully in appreciation of her petite but decidedly womanly curves.

A sigh escaped her lips as he began caressing both her breasts, tugging and teasing her hard nipples. She reminded him of the Russian instrument, the Balalaika, as he began playing with her virgin body—it would be so easy to pluck and strum her body into a beautiful frenzy.

Rytsar kissed her again, concentrating on the taste and feel of her mouth as his hand traveled lower, pulling the material of her skirt up so he could stroke her bare thigh.

Tatianna froze for a moment.

"I just want to touch you," he assured her as he resumed his passionate kissing.

She was too caught up in the chemistry flowing between them to deny him, and opened her legs wider.

Rytsar smiled as he kissed her more fervently. He barely grazed her wet cotton panties with his fingers and felt her entire body shudder in response.

His own libido became an inferno.

Tatianna looked down at the outline of his cock bulging against the material of his pants and became transfixed by it.

Rytsar didn't mind the attention and sat back in a more relaxed position. "Would you like to get acquainted?"

"*Da, pozhaluista.*"

Rytsar unbuckled his belt and unbuttoned his jeans for her. He then lay back with a mischievous grin and commanded, "Unzip my pants."

Tatianna sucked in her breath. He marveled at how attractive she was, so innocent and pure, but with that slight upturn of the lips that let him know that although she was inexperienced, she had an adventurous spirit.

Her hands trembled slightly from nerves as she unzipped his pants and pulled down the briefs to expose his naked shaft.

"You are allowed to touch it," he stated when she continued to stare at his cock without moving.

Tatianna tentatively reached out and laid her hand on his shaft. He closed his eyes for a moment as jolts of desire blurred his resolve.

"Can I kiss it?" she asked.

Rytsar opened his eyes again, unsure if he could handle the intimacy of her lips without ravaging her, but he was unwilling to say no.

"I want you to."

He grunted when her soft lips made contact with his rigid shaft.

"Do you like that?" she asked with a slight grin.

His cock released precum in answer and Rytsar smirked. "Lick it and find out."

Tatianna gazed back down at the head of his cock, glistening with his essence, and took a shy, inexperienced lick.

Fire rushed through his groin and he growled passionately.

Tatianna licked her lips afterward and arched her eyebrows.

"To your liking?" he asked casually.

"I have tasted nothing like it before...but yes, Anton. You taste good."

Her demure smile sent his libido into overdrive.

Lord help me...

"I would like to admire your naked body, *vorobyshek,*" he whispered in her ear, pulling at the waistband of her panties.

Her eyes grew wide, but Tatianna stood up and undid her skirt, letting it fall to the floor. She then slipped her fingers under the material and slowly pulled her panties down, showing off her dark curls and just the barest hint of her clit.

"You are even more beautiful than I envisioned," he said huskily, reaching out to her.

Tatianna took his hand, her gaze locked on to his as she hesitantly moved closer. His hands trailed over her skin and he wondered at the sheer smoothness of it.

Untouched, virgin territory...

Today would be her introduction to his loving caress.

Someday, after every part of her body had become accustomed to his passionate touch, Rytsar would acquaint her with the intimacy of his 'nines. He was certain the synergy of the exchange would prove life-altering for them both.

"You are truly exquisite, Tatianna," he said in awe. In all the years he'd enjoyed women, he'd never encountered an angel before.

Rytsar beckoned her to him, and gently stroked his fingers against her cheek.

Tatianna looked at him and smiled at him lovingly. "You are a handsome man, Anton."

He grunted, amazed that in all the countless times he'd heard that compliment from the lips of others, it had never affected him the way it was now.

Rytsar was certain this encounter would change him in a fundamental way. It was unnerving, yet he was unwilling to prevent it. "I am in love with this body," he told her.

"I am in love with this mind," she countered as she touched his forehead.

Rytsar grasped her head with both hands and lowered it so he could kiss her firmly on the top of the head. "What you do not realize, Tatianna, is that I will make sweet, sensual love to this mind. Every thought will become mine, not because I demand it, but because you will be hopelessly devoted to me."

Her eyes shone with the enthusiasm of young love, and she tentatively took his hand and placed it on her right breast. "Make love to me, Anton."

Rytsar had to check himself. What she was asking was exactly what his entire body ached to experience, but he could not succumb to the temptation.

Tatianna deserved to be swept off her feet, and that was exactly what he planned to do. After a day of being spoiled like a princess on her birthday, then—and only then—would he claim her virginity.

Rytsar took the Durov family ring off his pinky and slipped it onto her middle finger. "The day I ask for this ring back is the day I will make love to you, Tatianna. It is my solemn vow."

Tatianna stared at it, knowing its worth and significance to Rytsar. His grandfather had gifted him the ancestral ring, passing over his father and older brothers to do it. Although it had created animosity with his kin, Rytsar treasured this symbol of his grandfather's belief in him.

He was *not* a product of his current lineage—his reputation and destiny were his alone to forge.

Mollified by the gift, Tatianna did not beg to be taken again. Instead, she agreed to lie down on the couch so that he could admire her virginal pussy and take in its sweet scent. When she started to giggle, he looked up.

"Your breath, it tickles, Anton."

Rytsar surprised her by moving up from between her legs to plant a possessive kiss on her lips as he pressed his naked chest against hers.

"Our hearts beat as one," he growled possessively.

"Yes," she agreed, kissing him again.

His sixth sense alerted him to the fact someone was coming. Without wasting time to explain why, Rytsar got up and quickly handed Tatianna her clothes before he started dressing himself.

She shot him a questioning glance, but said nothing

as she hurriedly put on her clothes.

"Take the vodka and return with a glass of water," he commanded calmly.

Rytsar checked himself over to make sure nothing was amiss before sitting back down on the couch. He took a relaxed pose and called out to her, "Did Titov ever tell you about the time—"

The front door opened and her parents walked inside with the rest of their brood behind them just as Tatianna was coming out of the kitchen with a simple glass of water. It was obvious by the shocked look on their faces, everyone was surprised to see Rytsar there alone with Tatianna.

"What is the meaning of this!" her father sputtered.

"Papa!" Tatianna scolded him good-naturedly. "Poor Anton came to see Titov. How could he know my brother forgot he was coming today? I hated to turn him away without at least offering a glass of water." She lifted the glass to her father and smiled sweetly.

Her mother bought her explanation hook, line, and sinker.

"We apologize Titov was so rude to you, Anton," she said sadly. "He has not been himself these days. Please say you'll forgive our thoughtless son and stay for dinner."

Rytsar appreciated the offer. It would give him more time in Tatianna's presence and allow for some quality time with her father. He was determined to win the man over, despite the recent split with Titov.

He would do whatever it took to make sure Tatianna was his, because nothing could prevent a Durov from claiming his mate.

Alternate Plans

Rytsar awoke with a start. The formless dream quickly faded, leaving him only with a sense of urgency. He gently moved Brie from him and left the bed. Although it was predawn, Rytsar went out to swim in the ocean, trying to unravel what it was that his dream was pressing him to do.

Did it have to do with Thane, the Kozlov brothers, or the beast half-sister? He couldn't tell but, with each passing moment, the feeling of exigency grew stronger.

He was not surprised to see Titov waiting for him when he finally came back to shore. "What is it?" he asked, taking the robe offered him.

"They're here."

"The brothers," Rytsar stated rather than asked, already knowing he was correct.

"We just received news their men landed last night."

Rytsar played out what needed to be done with no time left. There were loose ends that must be tied up. He owed his brother that.

"You will take Mrs. Davis to the hospital this morning. There is someone I need to meet with before we leave the country."

"What about the captive?"

"Put extra men at the compound and put them on alert. They must be ready to move her at a moment's notice."

"Of course. Who do you want with you?"

"No one."

"Do you feel that's wise?"

"I don't want any of my people to get caught in the crossfire should Kozlov's men catch up with me."

Titov looked at Rytsar with a solemn expression. "I prefer to remain by your side."

Rytsar put his hand on Titov's shoulder. "No. I need you to protect what is most valuable to me."

Titov frowned but nodded his understanding.

"Is the apartment ready?"

"The equipment was delivered yesterday."

"Good. Keep a few guards here at the beach house on the pretense we are unaware of their arrival, but return Mrs. Davis's things to the apartment."

"What about the cat?"

Rytsar smirked. "What about the cat?"

"You will handle it?"

Rytsar rolled his eyes. "Only if I must."

"Good," Titov replied simply.

Rytsar was amused that his men were afraid of a mere cat, but would willingly face the Kozlov brothers to protect him.

"When I give the word, everyone disperses and makes their way back to Russia separately."

"But I stay with you," Titov insisted.

"No."

His look of distress was touching.

"I explained you would either come into riches or die for associating with me. I would prefer the first outcome for you."

Titov shifted uncomfortably.

"Fate is coming for me, comrade. I feel it in my bones. I choose to face it alone on my terms."

Titov looked him in the eye. "Understand that I will expect your return and will have a glass and bottle of vodka waiting on the table for you."

Rytsar smacked him on the back, laughing. "I look forward to toasting to your good fortune."

As they started toward the house, Titov stopped him. "I do not want this to be how it ends between us."

"Nor I," Rytsar assured him, "but we must be prepared."

Once inside, he made his way to the bedroom.

"Is something wrong, Rytsar?" Brie asked in the dim light once he closed the door.

Although he appreciated her intuitive nature, it was not welcomed now. "I must leave on an errand. Titov will be taking you to the hospital today."

"Is it Lilly?"

At least her question meant he did not have to lie to her. "No, I have a meeting with Marquis Gray."

"Marquis?" she asked in surprise. "Well, please tell him hello for me."

"Of course," Rytsar answered, barely listening to her—too busy formulating plans in his head as he entered the bathroom and started the water in the tub. "Now go back to sleep," he urged her, shutting the door before settling down into the hot water.

A few minutes later, he heard the door open. Brie was silent as she stepped into the tub and eased herself between his legs, laying her back against him.

Rytsar wrapped an arm around her to pull Brie closer. Closing his eyes, Rytsar concentrated on the relaxing heat of the bath water, the feel of her naked skin against his, and the synergy of their unspoken connection.

He grasped her throat to expose her neck and bit down, purposely leaving a mark. "I love you, *radost moya.*"

She turned her head and smiled as she rubbed the bite mark he'd left. "I love you too, Rytsar."

They remained in the tub in silent union, Rytsar refusing to stir until the water began to turn cold.

In life, all things must end.

He grunted as he helped her up and out of the tub. She took a towel off the rack and waited to dry him off. Brie was tender as she dried every inch of his skin.

Rytsar could tell that she was cherishing the moment, soaking up every detail of it. When she was finished, Brie stood up on her tiptoes and kissed him.

"A good-luck kiss for today."

He gave her a crooked smile. "If Thane asks for me, tell him I will see him soon."

Brie took his hand and interlaced it with hers. "I'm sure he'll understand. Will I see you tonight?"

"Of course," he assured her.

"Good, because I got the impression you're planning to leave us."

"Only if Fate is as cruel as I am," he answered. Rytsar grabbed the towel from her and snapped it on her ass to stop her from asking more questions.

She squealed in surprise. "Ow!"

"Get moving so your beautiful face is the first thing your man sees today."

Brie giggled, rubbing her ass cheek as she left him alone in the bathroom.

Rytsar looked at his reflection in the large mirror and felt a surge of power knowing what he had to do.

Rytsar called Marquis on his drive there, hoping the trainer would be open to the unexpected visit.

"What is the reason you wish to meet so early?" Marquis asked before agreeing.

"Mrs. Davis has an issue that I need you to take care of."

"Ah…the great mystery is about to be revealed to me," he surmised.

"Of all her friends, I felt you were the one I could trust with the responsibility."

"Did Brie agree to this?"

"There are things even she does not know."

Marquis paused for a moment before responding. "I'm unsure if I will be able to help, but I am willing to listen to your request."

"Good, I should be there in twenty."

"Celestia will have a pot brewing when you get here."

Rytsar didn't bother telling Marquis he only drank vodka in the morning.

He was shocked when the Wolfpup greeted him at

the door. "Why are you here?" he demanded, having never forgiven the boy for his arrogance.

"I live here," Faelan answered, moving aside so Rytsar could enter.

"Living with the parents. Fitting, I guess," Rytsar said in a dismissive tone as he made his way down the hallway.

"Mr. Durov, what an honor to have you join us this morning," Celestia said, giving him a quick bow before asking, "Do you like your coffee black or with cream and sugar?"

"Neither, but a shot of vodka in it would do nicely."

"Oh," she stated in surprise. "Well, I would be happy to get that for you."

As she was leaving, he added, "If you left out the coffee, that would be even better."

Celestia flashed him a smile as she left the room.

"Drinking so early?" Marquis asked as he walked into the room to join them.

"For some it dulls the senses. For me, it only enhances."

While the two men sat down next to each other, Faelan chose to remain standing.

"I did not expect the boy to be here," Rytsar complained to Marquis. "The news is not for his ears."

"Before you make that determination, I want you to know that Mr. Wallace is someone I have come to admire and trust. I do not say that lightly, as you know."

Rytsar glanced at Faelan and growled, "You know how I feel about you."

"And the feeling's mutual, I assure you," Faelan replied. "However, Marquis said that Brie is involved and needs help. If there is any way I can be of assistance, I would like to offer my services."

"Why would I let you have anything to do with Mrs. Davis, after the shit you pulled on them after the collaring?"

Faelan gave an exasperated sigh. "I understand you like to hold on to the past and have yet to open your eyes to the fact I have matured since then. Thane, Brie, and I have made our peace."

"I don't trust you. Tigers don't change their stripes."

"They can if they die and are reborn. As you are well aware, I have had such an experience and I tell you again, I have matured since."

Rytsar looked back at Marquis. "Would you trust this man with Brie's life?"

Marquis didn't hesitate. "Yes."

Rytsar growled under his breath. While he could appreciate the advantage of having two caretakers looking after Lilly, he did not like being beholden to the Wolfpup even though the boy might be better suited for the duty.

"What about your woman? I remember hearing you collared the blonde."

Faelan frowned. "She chose to leave."

Narrowing his eyes, Rytsar asked, "How can you be trusted around Brie if that is the case?"

"Thane trusted me enough to leave Brie behind to take care of me when I had the kidney transplant. So I guess you're the only one with the problem."

Rytsar snorted. "If Thane wasn't conscious, I would not even consider it. But now, if you make a misstep, you will have to answer to him."

"Did you say Mr. Davis is conscious?" Marquis questioned.

Rytsar turned to him. "Yes, it happened just yesterday. I suppose we were too busy celebrating to share the news with others."

"This is extraordinary!" Marquis exclaimed. "Celestia," he called out.

She hurried into the room and Marquis got up, holding out his hands to her. "Sir Davis is awake."

A smile spread across her face as she embraced her Master. "I can't believe it! This is wondrous news!"

"It is. It truly is."

Even Faelan was grinning and said, "I knew he would fight his way back. He's an even tougher bastard than I am."

"And you remember that, Wolfpup," Rytsar warned.

Marquis sent Celestia out of the room again and addressed Rytsar. "Why don't we get down to the reason you're here. You don't appear to have time to waste if I'm reading you right."

"True." Rytsar motioned for Faelan to sit. "I'll make this quick and to the point. Thane's half-sister plotted to kill Brie's baby and sell Brie into slavery. She came close, but Nosaka arrived in time to prevent the kidnapping."

Both men were silent for a moment, shocked by the revelation.

"What the hell? You can't be serious," Faelan demanded.

"She is behind bars now, I assume," Marquis stated.

Rytsar snorted angrily. "No, your authorities were unable to catch her and the threat was too great to allow the woman to be free. As soon as I arrived and was made aware of the situation, I took it upon myself to take care of it. It took a little time and persuasion, but she finally confessed."

Marquis stiffened. "Are you saying you kidnapped and tortured Thane's sister?"

"Half-sister, and no. I merely detained her and manipulated her living conditions. Since she carries a child, I was careful not to harm the fetus."

"She's pregnant?" Marquis questioned, sounding even more concerned.

"The woman is deranged. She was blackmailing Thane because she carried another man's child, but claimed it was Thane's after she drugged him in China."

"You have got to be fucking kidding me," Faelan exclaimed.

"I assure you I'm not. Her plan was to kill Mrs. Davis's child, and convince Thane that her own child was his so he would raise it as his own. But her level of madness goes even deeper. She is in love with him and planned to become intimate partners."

Marquis became somber as he listened to Rytsar. "This woman has serious psychiatric needs, Durov. She should be in the hospital, not under your 'care'."

"You do not appreciate the grave threat she poses to Brie. If the authorities were unable to arrest her, what makes you think a psych ward would be able to keep her from escaping?"

"I have more trust in our system than you," Marquis stated.

"And I have none," Rytsar shot back. "I guarantee you that she will harm Brie if she escapes, and she will remain a threat until her dying breath."

Marquis sat back for a moment, taking in what had been shared.

Faelan took the opportunity to ask Rytsar, "What is it you want us to do?"

"I may have to leave suddenly in the next day or two, but I must be assured the threat will remain contained."

"I will not participate in a kidnapping," Marquis informed him.

"So you will not help protect Brie?"

"I did not say that, but it must be done legally and through proper channels."

"What are you suggesting then?" Rytsar asked, trying to keep his irritation in check.

"Despite what you think, I do understand the danger she poses to both Brie and Sir Davis. Therefore, we must 'arrange' for the police to find and arrest her, and it must be in a neutral spot so you are not connected in any way. If she is already wanted by the police and as deranged as you say, even if they question her it is doubtful they will take anything she says seriously."

Rytsar chewed on his suggestion. Although it might work, he felt it wasn't enough and asked, "What if she escapes?"

Faelan spoke up. "I will do whatever it takes to protect Brie. You and I are alike in that way, Durov."

"Anything?" Rytsar pressed.

"I have nothing to lose and I owe Thane for every breath I take. He found my donor."

Just like with Nosaka, it seemed Rytsar might have misread the Wolfpup. It was not easy admitting when he was wrong, but his ego had no place in this situation.

"When the times comes, I will arrange for her to be deposited in the place we found her and have you alert the police to her location."

"That sounds acceptable," Marquis stated.

"But you have to swear on your life that she will not escape."

"I will swear," Faelan answered.

Marquis was not as quick to reply. "I promise I will do everything in my power to keep this woman behind bars—not only for Brie's sake, but for her own."

"How you could feel any shred of sympathy for her is beyond me," Rytsar snarled.

"Her actions speak to mental illness, not a conscious choice."

Rytsar shook his head angrily. "You live a sheltered life if you believe that."

"I can only speak to what I know," Marquis replied.

"I am speaking from experience," Rytsar answered.

Marquis bowed his head slightly. "I respect that."

Rytsar turned back to the Wolfpup. "I'm depending on you to fill in when the judicial system fails."

"I will be ready," Faelan assured him.

Rytsar stood up, ready to leave. "Give me a pen and paper to write down the address so you can burn it once you receive the call."

While Marquis went to get the items, Faelan spoke to Rytsar privately. "I am not afraid to get my hands dirty."

"Good, because brutality is the only language this creature understands."

Marquis came back. After calling Titov to get the location where his men had originally found her, Rytsar wrote down the address and handed it to him. "Then we are agreed. If you get the phone call, you will take care of the things we discussed."

"Yes."

"And everything I have shared stays between us."

"Naturally," Marquis answered.

"Of course," Faelan replied.

"Fine." Rytsar shook both their hands and turned to leave, stating, "I will see myself out."

He only made it halfway before Celestia caught up with him. "Mr. Durov, please. May I ask a favor of you?"

He turned around to see her holding a wrapped gift.

"Would you mind giving this to Thane? We're just so thrilled he's recovering. It's a prayer answered."

Rytsar took the gift from her. "I will make sure he gets it."

"Do you know if Brie plans to tell everyone soon or is this supposed to remain a secret for the time being?"

"I'm sure she plans on telling everyone, but I will ask her to call you so she can answer that herself."

"Thank you, Mr. Durov. It was an unexpected treat to see you today. I hope we will have the privilege again soon."

"If Fate allows, I hope that as well. Thank you, Celestia. You are a gracious hostess."

She smiled as she opened the door for him. "You simply couldn't have brought better news. Thank you."

Rytsar left knowing he had done all he could concerning Lilly. Now he was left to trust in Marquis's wisdom and Faelan's sense of loyalty.

Lost

R ytsar returned to the beach house to collect the cat.
There was a sense of emptiness that hadn't
been there before. It was echoed in the lonely howl that
came from under the leather sofa.

"It is time to go home," Rytsar stated.

He ran his hands over the cool marble of the kitchen
counters before opening the fridge and pulling out the
bag of cooked bacon. He'd used it every day since the cat
had joined them at the beach house.

Walking over to the big leather recliner, he sat down
and offered the cat a piece. It took a few minutes. The
black cat was still cautious around him, but it finally
emerged and sauntered over to Rytsar. It took the bacon
from his hand and lowered it to the floor, nibbling on it
slowly.

Reaching out his hand cautiously, Rytsar attempted
to pet the feline. It looked up, challenging him with its
stare.

Rytsar went for it anyway, and was gratified when the
beast closed its eyes and allowed him to stroke its black

fur.

"We must leave this place," Rytsar explained, feeling slightly foolish for talking to a cat, but compelled to do so just the same. The cat opened its eyes and seemed to stare straight into Rytsar's soul, sending a chill down his spine.

He cleared his throat and grabbed another piece of bacon, feeling disconcerted because of the cat. He held the bacon out to Shadow, but the cat ignored it, moving closer to rub against Rytsar's leg.

That had never happened before.

Rytsar wasn't sure what to make of it and actually gasped when the giant beast jumped from the floor onto his lap. He stayed stock-still, expecting it to either attack or bolt if he made any move.

The cat lay down across his thighs, its tail swishing back and forth slowly.

Rytsar was unnerved by its actions.

"Are you really going to let me pick you up and walk out of here? Because that was not the plan." He nodded to a blanket that had been laid out for the capture of the beast.

The cat raised its head to look at him, narrowing its eyes.

"If you escape while I'm walking to the car, Brie will never forgive me and I don't have time to chase you."

Going against his better judgment, Rytsar cautiously put his hands around the cat and lifted it up as he stood. Shadow didn't resist, although he refused to look at Rytsar. It was as if the cat was enduring this indignity.

Could Brie be right?

Maybe this animal *was* capable of some level of higher thinking. Regardless, Rytsar didn't have time to question his good fortune, and walked out the door to his car without incident.

The cat settled down on the passenger seat, its eyes closed but tail still twitching.

"You will only have to put up with me a little while longer, *kot*," Rytsar said with mock sympathy.

While he was driving, Rytsar noticed he was low on fuel. He groaned, but not having any other choice, he pulled into the next gas station and lectured the cat to remain put. He filled up the tank, despite the fact he would not be using the car for much longer.

Just as he was sliding into the driver's seat, an unknown assailant jumped into the back of the car, wrapping a cord around his neck.

Rytsar struggled unsuccessfully to free himself from the rope as it choked the life out of him.

It can't end like this...

Suddenly the vehicle erupted in inhuman howls as the black beast viciously attacked the face of his assailant. The instant Rytsar felt some slack, he broke free. He stumbled out of the car, falling to the ground gasping for breath while his attacker escaped.

The gas owner came running up to him. "I called the cops. You want me to call an ambulance too?"

Rytsar didn't want anything to do with the authorities and struggled to stand up. He waved the man off and got back into the car, speeding away as fast as he could.

When he finally caught his breath, he called Titov. "I need a new vehicle. I can't afford being stopped by the police over this."

"What happened?" Titov asked, concerned.

"I was attacked. I didn't see it coming."

"*Blyad'!*" Titov cursed.

"I'm certain the assassin was waiting at the beach house. Why I didn't pick up on it is beyond me." He looked at Shadow accusingly.

After Rytsar hung up the phone, he pointed at the cat. "This is your fault."

The cat stared him down.

"You may have saved my life, but I was distracted because of you."

The cat turned its head away.

He rubbed the sore area on his neck, shaken by the incident. It didn't appear the Kozlov brothers were taking prisoners. A few more miles down the road, Rytsar had a change of heart and reached out to lightly pet Shadow's head. "Thank you."

The cat answered his gratitude by crawling over the middle console and into his lap, making it harder to drive, but Rytsar didn't try to push him away. He looked down at the huge animal, humbled by the fact he owed a cat for his life.

It seemed time had finally run out.

Rytsar stood naked in Thane's apartment, facing the window with his hands raised on either side. He was lost in the music of "O Fortuna", having turned the volume high so he could become oblivious of his surroundings.

Despite that, he was well aware when Brie entered the apartment alone, his senses having been heightened after his recent near-death experience.

"Rytsar, what's wrong?" Brie yelled over the music as she approached.

He lowered his arms and turned to her.

Brie cried out when she saw the nasty mark around his neck. "What happened to you?"

"There is nothing more to be done, *radost moya*."

"What are you talking about? Who did this to you?"

"I always knew there would be a price to be paid, and I have no regrets."

"What price? Who wants you dead? I don't understand."

Rytsar pulled her close and sang the powerful last words of the song to her, "Since Fate strikes down the strong man…Everyone weep with me."

Brie stiffened in his arms, shaking her head. "No…"

He let her go to turn off the music before returning to her.

"Tell me who wants you dead?" she whimpered.

"I must pay for the death of the maggot."

"That horrible man in Russia?"

Rytsar nodded. "His relations are dangerous people, *radost moya*. I had hoped to avoid capture, but that hope has vanished now. I cannot stay or I risk your life as well."

She traced the angry red line on his neck. "How did you get away?"

Rytsar glanced at the cat sitting on the arm of the

sofa. "Your feline protector." He snorted. "Do you think I owe it caviar and catnip for the rest of its life?"

Brie wrapped her arms around him and started to cry. "Rytsar, I can't stand the thought of what almost happened."

He felt her fear and desperation, and longed to comfort her but he had none to give.

"You must promise me one thing."

She stepped away from him, frowning through her tears. "I won't make any promises."

"You must," he insisted. He held out his hands and beckoned her back to him.

She reluctantly returned, sobbing against his chest.

Rytsar leaned down and spoke to her in a calm, even voice. "Your life will be forfeit if you do not keep this promise, *radost moya.*"

She tried to pull away, but he held her even tighter.

"They will not stop until I am dead. If the worst happens, you must promise not to intervene. If you fail in that, they will kill you without hesitation. Promise me you will do that," he demanded.

She shook her head, sobbing quietly.

"Promise me."

She shook her head.

Rytsar cupped her chin. "I cannot leave unless I know you are okay. Nothing else matters to me."

"What about Sir? How can you abandon him without a fight?"

He gazed intently into those honey-colored eyes. "Know that I have done everything possible to prevent this. But there comes a point when one must succumb to

Fate or endanger the ones they love."

Her lip trembled. "I can't lose you."

"I am with you always. Did we not make the blood-bond?" he asked, grasping her wrist and turning it to show the newly formed scar.

"Sir and I don't want a scar—we want you."

Rytsar grasped her shoulders and shook her, growling. "Enough!"

Brie grabbed him, wrapping herself around his waist, crying, "No, you don't get to cut me out of your life."

He looked down at her with an overwhelming sense of tenderness. He'd always known life was cruel—it was a repeating lesson in his life. She, on the other hand, was just getting a taste of how merciless Fate could be. He didn't want that for her, and hated that he was the cause.

Rytsar enveloped her in his arms again and let down his defenses, allowing the tears to fall—tears of frustration, tears of rage, and tears of loss.

Brie pressed against him, losing herself in his sorrow. Eventually the tears stopped, and he was himself again.

Pulling away from her, he told her, "There's nothing more you can do for me other than to keep your promise." He turned away from her and started toward the guest bedroom.

"Rytsar," she called out.

He turned around to face her.

"What do you need—tonight?"

"Just keep your promise."

He walked into the bedroom and shut the door. He settled into bed knowing there would be no sleep for him. After several minutes, he heard a light knock on the door.

"Go away," he barked.

Brie ignored his order and opened the door, letting the light shine in. Rytsar could see her naked frame in the doorway.

"I spoke to Sir." She walked inside and shut the door, shrouding them in darkness again. "He told me to love you well."

Tears pricked his eyes. "Then come to me, *radost mo-ya.*"

Rytsar took her in his arms and they lay in silence, his heart breaking over a memory that still haunted him to this day. "I have a strange request. You are not obligated to say yes."

Brie rested her chin on his chest. "Rytsar, it would be my pleasure. Anything…"

He put his finger on her lips. "Do not agree until you hear what it is I'm asking."

She nodded, and he took his finger away.

Rytsar said nothing at first as the memory of his last time with Tatianna flooded his mind. That stolen moment before their whole world was torn apart.

Finally he spoke. "I have one regret in my life."

"What is it?"

He leaned forward and kissed her forehead. "I never had the chance to make love to Tatianna. I made her a vow…"

Rytsar felt Brie's gentle hand on his face. "What do you need from me, Anton?"

Brie had used his given name, releasing a rush of un-expected emotions he was unprepared for. He turned his head away. Taking several deep breaths, he voiced out loud his need to her.

"I want to make love to Tatianna like I vowed—before her innocence was ripped away from her..." His voice caught. "I understand how odd that must sound to you."

"Not at all," Brie's voice assured him in the dark. "I would be honored to be your vessel."

"This would not be role play. You would not be allowed to speak, only to receive."

Brie nodded as she brushed her hand against his jaw. "I understand."

Rytsar closed his eyes again, crying out to the heavens.

Oh Tatianna, how I've missed you...

Rytsar took off his ring and slid it onto Brie's finger, kissing her hand and saying tenderly, "Stay here, *vorobyshek*."

He exited the room and gathered a couple of items from Thane's closet before returning to her. Rytsar placed the large candles on the nightstand and lit them, satisfied with the subtle light they provided.

He then turned to face Brie.

In his mind's eye, he saw his beautiful Tatianna before him and a tear escaped as he held out his hand to her. "Tatianna, our time has finally come..."

She came to him, pressing her cheek against his chest

as he wrapped his protective arms around her. He held her for a long time, content simply to be in her presence again.

When he felt light gentle kisses on his chest, he cupped her chin and lifted her head up to stare into those deep blue eyes. They still held the innocence and youthful love he remembered so well…

Rytsar took Tatianna's hand and played with the ring on her finger. "Do you remember when I gave you this ring?"

She nodded, her eyes sparkling with delight.

"I would like it back now." He slowly slid the ring from her finger and placed it back on his pinky. "Because tonight, my Russian princess, I make love to you."

Her eyes glistened in the candlelight as he leaned down to kiss her perfect lips.

Suddenly, the horrifying image of her body, bloody and beaten, invaded his thoughts. In an instant, he was back to that moment of deep-seated pain when he'd finally found her after months of searching—his beautiful virgin violated and broken by the unholy.

"I'm sorry, Tatianna…" he choked out in grief and guilt.

She shook her head, placing her finger on his lips. When she removed it, she gave him a tender kiss and smiled. Her kiss held no anger or resentment, communicating only her devotion to him.

"You own my soul, little sparrow."

She traced her fingers over his heart.

Pressing her small frame against his body, he held her. He needed a few moments before beginning his seduction.

"I have a confession to make," he whispered huskily. "I would have made love to you that day if your parents hadn't interrupted us."

She giggled underneath him, kissing his chin playfully.

Rytsar growled as he moved her head to the side so he could kiss her neck as his hands slowly explored her naked body. She giggled when he found the sensitive area on her stomach that made her jump as his hand traveled down farther to rest just above her mound.

He would be thoughtful and gentle with his taking of her. Rytsar wanted to express the powerful love he felt in his caress. He needed Tatianna to experience the magic known only to lovers when bodies and souls connect.

Rytsar literally spent hours exploring, tasting and teasing her, building up Tatianna's desire for that moment when he took her virginity and their souls melded as one.

The pain she would feel would pale in comparison to the passion he would coax from her. When he felt she was ready, he lay between her legs and looked down at her.

"Do you know how beautiful you are?"

Her arched eyebrows, so expressive and feminine, teased his masculine sensibilities as she looked at him with pure adoration.

Rytsar positioned his shaft against her wet, untouched opening. "I love you," he told her as he began to press his cock into her. Her gaze never left his, and she made no sound as she took in his hard shaft.

With slow strokes, he made love to her. As Tatianna's body grew accustomed to his length, he was able to increase the intensity of his thrusts. He kissed her deeply, wanting her to associate the act of fucking with the intimacy it inspired.

The moment when she instinctually arched her back to receive more of his cock was powerful and significant. He pressed his lips against her neck and bit down, claiming her as his mate. Tatianna cried out in passion and pain, shuddering as she came for the first time.

Rytsar ached to join her in release but he held back, knowing there was so much more he needed to share. An entire night of lovemaking would not be enough to adequately express the depth and intensity of his love for her, but he was determined to try.

As dawn broke over the horizon, Rytsar leaned down to kiss her beautiful breasts, his spent cock buried deep inside her. He tenderly moved a stray curl from her face, glistening with sweat.

This time it wasn't Tatianna, but Brie whom he saw. "I love you, *radost moya*."

A lone tear ran down her cheek as she leaned up to kiss him.

"Thank you for last night," he said gruffly as he rolled from her body to lie beside her on the bed.

She took his hand and intertwined her fingers with his.

The simple gesture touched him and he lifted their entwined hands, smiling to himself.

Rytsar felt lighter of spirit, as if Tatianna had truly been with him during the night. He was a stronger man for it—and was ready to face what lay ahead.

His Vow

Rytsar entered the hospital room with Brie at his side. He held out his hand to Thane and shook it firmly. "Thank you, *moy droog*. You cannot know what that meant to me."

Thane nodded, glancing at Brie and motioning her to him. Shaking with effort, he took her hand and turned it palm side up, kissing it tenderly. He noticed the fresh scar on her wrist and then looked at Rytsar.

Rytsar spoke up before he even asked. "Yes, I made the vow of fidelity and protection with her, as I did with you eighteen years ago, brother," he answered, showing his matching wrist.

Thane looked up at Brie and with difficulty, turned his own wrist over to show off his old scar on his left arm, and smiled at her with warmth in his eyes.

Brie broke down in tears, wrapping her arms around Thane, kissing him first on the lips and then over every exposed surface. "I love you so much, Sir, it hurts."

Thane turned his attention back on Rytsar. With great effort he said, "I can't…lose you."

Rytsar frowned, placing his hand on Sir's chest. "Nor I you, comrade. You must vow to do nothing. If they do not ascertain a threat, they will have no reason to kill you."

Thane shook his head.

"You must. They will eliminate you without hesitation."

He continued to stare defiantly at Rytsar.

"Who will be left to raise the babe?"

A pained expression flashed across Thane's eyes, and he glanced at Brie again. Rytsar could tell his brother was struggling with the cold reality of the situation they faced.

Rytsar clasped his hand. "I have accepted my fate, but it cannot be yours."

Brie cried out, "I wish we'd never gone to your club that night."

"I have no regrets, *radost moya*. An innocent girl was saved. Rejoice with me that I am able to die a guiltless man."

Her bottom lip trembled and she turned from him, trying to rein in her emotions. Rytsar took solace that she cared so much, but tears would only make it harder for him.

"Is there really nothing we can do?" she finally asked when she could face him again.

"Let me go when the time comes."

Thane shook his head, still rejecting this unwanted reality.

Not wanting to waste time on things that could not be changed, Rytsar began to reminisce. "I think back to that boy I met in college…" Rytsar smiled impishly at Thane, adding, "What a social misfit."

Thane frowned, but Rytsar saw a hint of amusement behind his expression.

"If it hadn't been for a certain lively rebuttal you had with the philosophy professor, I would never have befriended such an utter nerd."

Thane croaked out the words, "Pompous…ass."

Rytsar laughed. "Me or the professor?"

Thane raised an eyebrow.

Rytsar shook his head, tsking. "Such blatant disrespect shown to the man you owe everything to. If it weren't for me, your peasant ass would have graduated with honors, and you would have wasted your life away in an office—missing out on the very best life has to offer." He gestured to Brie and kissed the air toward her.

Thane glanced at his woman, staring at her thoughtfully.

Rytsar slapped him on the shoulder. "We found out that tragedy can make the strangest of bedfellows, did we not? Who knew there was another man out there with as much emotional baggage as me?"

Thane chuckled softly.

"You may be exceptionally guarded, calculating and demanding, but your saving grace is that you are a very generous man. The fact you shared your one prized possession with me—for that I am eternally grateful."

Thane looked at him knowingly and nodded.

Rytsar took Brie by surprise, lifting her into the air, and saying passionately, "*Ya obozhayu tebya.*"

"We both…do…babygirl," Thane said gruffly.

Brie shook her head with a shy smile. "I don't know what that means."

Rytsar leaned down and mouthed the words, "I adore you."

She blushed sweetly, grinning at them both.

"But seriously, *moy droog,* the greatest gift of all is this." Rytsar whipped out his phone and hit the play button. The clear sound of the babe's quick heartbeat filled the room, infusing Rytsar with a deep sense of hope.

Tears came to Thane's eyes as he listened to it.

"No matter what Fate brings us, life will go on. It is a miraculous thing."

Thane nodded, holding out a shaking hand to Rytsar.

Suddenly there were screams out in the hallway.

"*Blyad'*, they're here. I never thought they would storm the hospital." He whipped out his phone and sent the prewritten warning "*daleko*" to his men, knowing they would carry out his plans. He then looked to Thane and commanded, "Close your eyes."

He reached in his pocket and pulled out a small piece of paper, pushing it into Brie's hand while murmuring under his breath, "Eyes to the floor, *radost moya.*"

Rytsar turned to face the door. For a moment, time seemed to stand still as he waited to meet his fate. The sound of his heartbeat filled his ears—slow, steady, and even.

Life is a strange series of events, he thought. *Pushing a person forward to meet up with destiny.*

Rytsar felt no fear as the four men entered the room with guns raised.

"Durov!"

He held up his hands in surrender.

"Don't make a move or everyone here will die," the leader of the four warned.

Rytsar noticed one of the men playing with the trigger on his gun as he stared at Brie. It was obvious the cretin was itching for a kill.

To distract him, Rytsar growled angrily, "Only weaklings work for the Kozlov brothers."

The man took the bait, holstering his gun to throw a hard right in Rytsar's face.

He took it without flinching, even smiling afterward, which only infuriated the man and invited several more furious blows. Rytsar grunted as his knees gave way and he fell to the floor, the sound of blood rushing to his head as the darkness crept in.

"Look at you," his attacker said, laughing cruelly. "Hiding in a hospital like the coward you are to avoid us." He kicked Rytsar in the ribs for added insult.

"Enough!" the leader said. "We've wasted too much time here."

"What about these two?"

Low, sarcastic laughter filled the room. "What, you mean that invalid and the sniveling cunt? Not worth the bullets to take them out."

Rytsar felt hands on him as he was dragged out of the hospital room. The sound of Brie quietly crying behind him was cause for rejoicing.

He had succeeded in protecting her, and Thane was alive and recovering.

That knowledge allowed Rytsar to relax as he was

shoved into the waiting van outside, as the police sirens closed in.

With the song "O Fortuna" ringing in his mind, Rytsar lifted his head up and attempted a smile, tasting the blood from his broken lip. He laughed at the pain as the van careened toward his destiny. Rather than kill him, he was being delivered into the hands of the enemy.

A crack to the skull from the butt of a gun ended his reverie and he sank into the black abyss. But as the darkness closed in around him, the promise he'd written on the note Brie now held in her hand flashed in his mind.

It was his solemn vow.

Tell moye solntse to save a dance for me. ~Anton

Thank you so much for reading. I hope you enjoyed the reading Her Russian Knight. The story continues in Under His Protection.

COMING NEXT

Under His Protection: Brie's Submission

14th Book in the Series

Available Now

Reviews mean the world to me!

I truly appreciate you taking the time to review
Her Russian Knight.

If you could leave a review on both Goodreads and the
site where you purchased this eBook from, I would be so
grateful. Sincerely, ~Red

If you are looking for more of Rytsar, my upcoming
release *The Russian Unleashed* in July 2020 features Rytsar

The Russian Unleashed

Rytsar Durov – Fine vodka with a side of sadism.

Young, rich, and in charge, Rytsar is ready to take on the
world.

Although his heart has been wounded, it still beats with a
passion that can't be contained.

ABOUT THE AUTHOR

Over Two Million readers have enjoyed Red's stories

Red Phoenix – USA Today Bestselling Author
Winner of 8 Readers' Choice Awards

Hey Everyone!

I'm Red Phoenix, an author who also happens to be a submissive in real life. I wrote the Brie's Submission series because I wanted people everywhere to know just how much fun BDSM can be.

There is a huge cast of characters who are part of Brie's journey. The further you read into the story the more you learn about each one. I hope you grow to love Brie and the gang as much as I do.

They've become like family.

When I'm not writing, you can find me online with readers.

I heart my fans! ~Red

To find out more visit my Website

redphoenixauthor.com

Follow Me on BookBub

bookbub.com/authors/red-phoenix

Newsletter: Sign up

redphoenixauthor.com/newsletter-signup

Facebook: AuthorRedPhoenix

Twitter: @redphoenix69

Instagram: RedPhoenixAuthor

I invite you to join my reader Group!

facebook.com/groups/539875076052037

SIGN UP FOR MY NEWSLETTER
HERE FOR THE LATEST RED
PHOENIX UPDATES

FOLLOW ME ON INSTAGRAM
INSTAGRAM.COM/REDPHOENIXAUTHOR

SALES, GIVEAWAYS, NEW
RELEASES, PREORDER LINKS, AND
MORE!
SIGN UP HERE
REDPHOENIXAUTHOR.COM/NEWSLETTER-
SIGNUP

Red Phoenix is the author of:

Brie's Submission Series:
Teach Me #1
Love Me #2
Catch Me #3
Try Me #4
Protect Me #5
Hold Me #6
Surprise Me #7
Trust Me #8
Claim Me #9
Enchant Me #10
A Cowboy's Heart #11
Breathe with Me #12
Her Russian Knight #13
Under His Protection #14
Her Russian Returns #15
In Sir's Arms #16
Bound by Love #17
Tied to Hope #18
Hope's First Christmas #19
Secrets of the Heart #20

*You can also purchase the AUDIO BOOK **Versions**

Also part of the Submissive Training Center world:

Rise of the Dominates Trilogy
Sir's Rise #1
Master's Fate #2
The Russian Reborn #3

Captain's Duet
Safe Haven #1
Destined to Dominate #2

The Russian Unleashed #1

Other Books by Red Phoenix

Blissfully Undone
* Available in eBook and paperback

(Snowy Fun—Two people find themselves snowbound in a cabin where hidden love can flourish, taking one couple on a sensual journey into ménage à trois)

His Scottish Pet: Dom of the Ages
* Available in eBook and paperback

Audio Book: *His Scottish Pet: Dom of the Ages*

(Scottish Dom—A sexy Dom escapes to Scotland in the late 1400s. He encounters a waif who has the potential to free him from his tragic curse)

The Erotic Love Story of Amy and Troy
* Available in eBook and paperback

(Sexual Adventures—True love reigns, but fate continually throws Troy and Amy into the arms of others)

eBooks

Varick: The Reckoning

(Savory Vampire—A dark, sexy vampire story. The hero navigates the dangerous world he has been thrust into with lusty passion and a pure heart)

Keeper of the Wolf Clan (Keeper of Wolves, #1)

(Sexual Secrets—A virginal werewolf must act as the clan's mysterious Keeper)

The Keeper Finds Her Mate (Keeper of Wolves, #2)

(Second Chances—A young she-wolf must choose between old ties or new beginnings)

The Keeper Unites the Alphas (Keeper of Wolves, #3)

(Serious Consequences—The young she-wolf is captured by the rival clan)

Boxed Set: Keeper of Wolves Series (Books 1-3)

(Surprising Secrets—A secret so shocking it will rock Layla's world. The young she-wolf is put in a position of being able to save her werewolf clan or becoming the reason for its destruction)

Socrates Inspires Cherry to Blossom

(Satisfying Surrender—A mature and curvaceous woman becomes fascinated by an online Dom who has much to teach her)

By the Light of the Scottish Moon

(Saving Love—Two lost souls, the Moon, a werewolf, and a death wish…)

In 9 Days

(Sweet Romance—A young girl falls in love with the new student, nicknamed "the Freak")

9 Days and Counting

(Sacrificial Love—The sequel to *In 9 Days* delves into the emotional reunion of two longtime lovers)

And Then He Saved Me

(Saving Tenderness—When a young girl tries to kill herself, a man of great character intervenes with a love that heals)

Connect with Red on Substance B

Substance B is a platform for independent authors to directly connect with their readers. Please visit Red's Substance B page where you can:

- Sign up for Red's newsletter
- Send a message to Red
- See all platforms where Red's books are sold

Visit Substance B today to learn more about your favorite independent authors.

Made in the USA
Monee, IL
23 September 2020

42525336R00144